WINNING HIS VOTE

AN ENEMIES TO LOVERS MM ROMANCE

CASEY MORALES

Edited by
CARLIE SLATTERY

1

ELECTION DAY

JOE

Nobody thought we could win.

I'd only given us a one-in-ten shot when the campaign began—but there we were, marching toward a historic victory.

Election Day had finally arrived, and our team was a beehive, buzzing with nervous anticipation. One local news station ran a poll over the weekend showing us ahead by more than twelve points, but anyone with campaign experience knew the only poll that mattered was the one conducted at the ballot box.

On cue, Marcus and his wife, Maria, held up their folded papers, waited for the cameras to snap, then dropped them into the thin slots on top of the boxes colored red and blue. They waved and flashed bright smiles. Few people knew the scene was a made-for-the-cameras sham. Voting in the state had been electronic for more than twenty years. Literally *no one* dropped a ballot in a box—except candidates who wanted to look good on TV or in the papers.

Marcus and Maria looked better than good.

They looked like winners.

"You two are doing great, really. We only have two more stops before the polls close."

Maria gave me a sidelong glance. "How are you so calm, Joe? I thought I was going to pass out before those cameras stopped clicking."

I squeezed her arm. "That's my job, ma'am. The cameras may be on you two, but the reporters are watching me for a reaction. If I show nerves, they start digging, wondering what's wrong within our camp."

She nodded weakly. We'd had this same conversation dozens of times, but I didn't think she ever fully bought it.

I leaned in and whispered, "If it helps, I've felt like I was about to pee all over myself for ten months."

Her full-throated laugh startled Marcus and seemed to release some of her tension. She gave me a quick hug. "You're too much, Joe. You know that?"

Marcus had been shaking voters' hands leaving the polling station, but never missed anything. He turned and gave me a warm smile. "She's got a point, but we're glad for it. In case I forget to say it later tonight, thank you for all you've done for us. I don't think I've ever seen anyone work so hard."

"Mayor, you've worked harder—"

He held up a palm. "I'm not mayor yet…but thanks."

Marcus smiled before returning his attention to the voters flowing into line from the parking lot. It was a heavy turnout. Was that good for us—or for them? Either way, there was nothing to be done now. We were only a few hours from the finish line.

For those of us in the campaigning profession, Election Day was strange. It felt eternal, like it'd never end. There were always more hands to shake, more voters to drive to the polls, more signs to post or ads to run. The list was endless—and somehow, as exhausted and relieved as we were when Election Day finally came to a close, we always wished we'd had more time.

We said our goodbyes to two older couples waving Sanchez for Mayor signs just outside the hundred-foot boundary, then drove to the next polling place.

BACK AT THE HOTEL, MARCUS AND MARIA SAT ON the couch, arms wrapped around each other. The adrenaline of the day had worn off and they were running on fumes. We all were.

I sat across from them, slumped into an over-stuffed chair.

The polls had just closed.

"What do you think?" Marcus finally asked. Maria's gaze held apprehension—and hope.

The silence of the room was deafening.

"I think we did our best." That was such a terrible answer, but it was the truth.

Marcus snorted. This was his first race, and he'd punched above his weight, vying to become the first Latino mayor the city had ever elected. The incumbent mayor was wildly popular and had ruled with an iron fist for two terms. If he won, he would be the first mayor to win a third term. There was a lot on the line for everyone.

I still remember a couple reporters in the back of the gaggle snickering as Marcus announced his candidacy. It had to be a joke, they said. No one could beat *the don*, especially not Marcus *Sanchez*. They mocked his ethnicity with insolent accents, egging each other on with sharp elbows and sharper laughs. I was sure they thought no one could hear them.

But I did—though I never told Marcus.

He'd faced worse jabs throughout his life, and I

couldn't shelter him from what promised to be a brutal campaign, but I shielded him from those on that day.

Raised in the northeastern quarter of the city, where crime was still winning its undeclared war, Marcus rose as a beacon of hope for a community bereft of such luxury. His parents were murdered when he was a teenager, victims of a robbery that netted forty-two dollars from his father's wallet, and a pair of worthless cubic zirconia earrings his mother wore. The murders were never solved, and Marcus ended up living with his ancient grandmother. She loved him fiercely, but was on the brink of needing care herself. The rudderless boy raised himself.

At fifteen, he started working in the local grocery mart as a bag clerk. The job didn't pay much, but it likely saved his life. Boys at school with their after-noons free found themselves in gangs, then grave-yards. Working every day after school insulated Marcus from the city's worst elements and taught him the ethics of service and sweat.

By seventeen, the mart's owner relied on him to run the store when he was away.

Maria stumbled into Marcus—literally—as he was stocking a display of boxed pasta. He lost his balance and hundreds of boxes of ziti flew across the mart's polished floors. They were married fourteen months later. She insisted they serve baked ziti at their rehearsal dinner.

The mart's owner died when Marcus was twenty-two. A single man without family or heirs, he left everything to the boy who'd become like a son. Between Maria's mind for numbers and Marcus's work ethic, the pair were unstoppable. By thirty, the Sanchez Grocery chain boasted three stores. Five more would follow before public service called.

He was a good man intent on doing good things.

When he offered me the job as his campaign manager, I was stunned. We'd talked about me doing opposition research or strategy work, but never taking the top spot.

I demanded brutal honesty with candidates, so I owed him my own. "Marcus, it's one thing to have gays supporting your campaign, but to have one running it will reflect on you. I guarantee *the don* will use it as a slur to gin up his base. This race is going to get ugly, and you shouldn't hand the other side ammo."

He didn't flinch. His eyes never wavered. "Joe, nobody thinks we can win anyway. Why do we care what they say? Besides, you're willing to support *me*, a guy who doesn't look like any mayor this city's ever had. How could I not support *you*?"

I could still feel the lump that had risen in my

throat as I searched his eyes for doubts that day. There were none. We shook hands and never looked back.

———

AN HOUR LATER, WE STOOD BUNCHED UP IN A hallway outside the campaign's election night party ballroom. Hundreds of supporters ate, drank, and watched televisions scattered throughout the hall for updates on the vote count. The crowd's tension slammed against the door like a battering ram.

My hand rested on the doorknob. I couldn't stop my fingers from playing trumpet notes across its brass. I wanted to throw up.

"Are we still ahead? What's happening?" Maria danced beside me.

"Hon, he doesn't know any more than we do. Take a breath." Marcus pecked her cheek and grinned.

"Actually, sir, ninety-four percent have reported in. We're up by nine percent. Given the precincts left, the result is likely to be called any minute."

"Seriously?" Maria hopped several times, unable to contain herself.

I grinned. "Yes, ma'am—or should I say, Madam First Lady of Nashville?"

"Elect," Marcus interjected.

We both turned to him.

"Madam First Lady of Nashville elect. We haven't been sworn in yet." His mouth quirked, and his eyes glittered.

Maria slapped his arm and laughed. "Oh, Marcus. You're impossible."

Before I could say anything, an announcement quieted the crowd. "Everybody, quiet. Channel Four is calling it."

Televisions were all tuned to Channel Four and cranked up to maximum volume: "Our decision desk is officially calling the mayoral race for Marcus Sanchez, the first Latino mayor in Nashville's history."

The crowd erupted, and pre-selected patriotic music blasted. Marcus and Maria embraced, and I had to fight back tears. My cell vibrated, and a text gave me the countdown.

"Marcus, Maria, two minutes," I said, sucking down my own excitement. "Mr. Mayor-elect, are you ready? It's the good speech. Please don't do your concession by accident."

Maria barked a giddy laugh. Marcus gripped my shoulders with both hands and pulled me into a tight hug. He was liberal with his praise, but the man never touched anyone who wasn't named Maria. His gesture destroyed the last of my defense, and an ugly-cry of epic proportions flowed faster than the drinks in the ballroom.

Maria's hand was on my face with a tissue in a flash. "What am I going to do with you two? Come here, Joe. You look a wreck." Her voice was filled with affection that had the opposite effect she'd sought. Before I knew it, I was wrapped in a three-way hug with the city's next mayor and his indomitable wife.

My phone buzzed again.

"It's time," I said as I wiped my face and gripped the door handle. "Give 'em hell, Mr. Mayor."

I pulled the door open and a familiar voice whipped the crowd into a frenzy. "Ladies and gentle-men, it is my pleasure to introduce the next mayor of Music City, USA, Marcus Sanchez!"

My heart leapt as Marcus and Maria stepped into the spotlight and waved to their supporters. The crowd roared louder, and again, I fought back tears. I couldn't rip my eyes away.

"Holy shit, we did it."

My head snapped around to find Pete Cabrea, one of our senior campaign staff and my best friend. He was all teeth and wide eyes as he pulled me into a jittery, over-caffeinated hug.

"Fuck yeah, we did! The good guys finally won one."

He laughed and pulled back, keeping his arm around my shoulders as we watched the Sanchez victory unfurl on stage. A moment later, as Marcus launched into his acceptance speech, Pete leaned over and whispered, "Who the fuck's that on stage with them?"

"Huh? Who?"

"The hot guy in the light blue shirt with his sleeves rolled up. Look at those forearms…and that ass. Damn."

I snorted. Pete was like a fritzed-out submarine periscope, stuck in the raised position and constantly swiveling when anything male ventured nearby. Any man with pecs, arms, or dimples—basically any man breathing—loaded his torpedo bays (or whatever the naval equivalent to an overheated sailor should be).

I knew who he was ogling, but glanced up anyway. The man standing a step behind and to the left of the podium towered over the Sanchezes at nearly six-foot-four. His sandy blond hair that looked like it wanted to curl was cropped short. His bright gray eyes never settled in one place as they danced from one cheering spectator to the next. I'd lost track of the number of times I'd heard people say they felt like the only person in the world when those eyes settled on theirs. Pete hadn't been wrong. The light blue dress shirt clinging to the man's chest left little question about his athleticism.

"You mean *Congressman* David Reese?"

"No shit. Really?"

I nodded.

"Damn. I didn't know we had a hot congressman. Does he need campaign staff? I've got a hard one—"

"Pete! Can we listen to Marcus?" I feigned annoyance, but couldn't stop a grin from forming. Nothing could dampen my mood, and Pete had a way of always making me laugh.

After an all-too-brief moment of silence, Pete asked, "What's a congressman doing introducing a newly elected mayor? Isn't that below his pay grade?"

I leaned over and whispered conspiratorially, "Not if said congressman plans to run for governor."

Pete's brows rose, and his eyes drank in Reese with new appreciation.

Marcus transitioned his speech from thank-yous to first steps he planned to take once sworn in. We'd heard these points at every rally and rubber-chicken dinner for ten months. Somehow, they never got old.

"How many times have you heard this speech? Come on, look at Representative Rumpalicious."

I hadn't expected that, and any composure I had left vanished. I had to step away from the door to keep my laughter from being heard onstage. When I gathered myself and turned back, the good congressman's eyes were locked onto us.

"Stare all you want. He might've been Mr. May in the Congressional Hottie Calendar last year, but I heard Congressman Reese is a real asshole. I worked with his staff to get him here tonight, so I can neither confirm nor deny any of that."

Pete was undeterred and blurted a little too loudly, "Asshole or not, he's delicious."

"Shit. I think he heard you." I winced and turned away from the stage again, giggling like a kid hearing a fart joke.

Pete stepped back and gave me a mocking bow. "I'm here to serve. Have fun tonight. I'm going to get smashing drunk."

As quickly as he'd snuck up on me, Pete vanished down the hallway. He reappeared a moment later in the back of the ballroom, weaving his way toward the open bar. I shook my head as he walked away with a glass of something in both hands. Lord help the hotel staff when this night was over.

When I turned back to watch the rest of the speech, Marcus and Maria stood a step behind the podium, hands clasped and raised toward the ceiling. The crowd was a writhing mass of excitement, drunk on victory and alcohol. Everyone I could see laughed and cheered, elated at the prospect of a brighter future.

Balloons fell on cue, turning the ballroom into a dance floor of motion, color, and light.

That's when I noticed Congressman Reese. He remained a step behind my candidate, but his face held none of the enthusiasm of those before him. His head moved slowly as he surveyed the crowd, his chin turned slightly upward. He couldn't look like more of an ass than he did in that moment.

Disgusted by his snobbish demeanor in Marcus's moment of triumph, my eyes chose to look elsewhere. They roamed his chest, now clearly visible under his dress shirt—more so for the lack of an undershirt— then traveled down his arms to the light hair of his forearms. The stage lighting hit his backside at just the right angle to make his tight dress pants practically glow.

What are you doing, idiot? He's a congressman— and a pompous ass. I laughed at myself, then turned to join the crowd's celebration, but I couldn't stop myself from giving Reese's butt one last glance before rounding the corner.

2

———

THE TRANSITION

JOE

There were only three months between Election Day and when Marcus would take office. A million details demanded attention, decisions and appointments to make, and most of them required the personal stamp of the mayor-elect. I hadn't planned on working past Election Day, but there was no way to refuse Maria when she asked me to help. That woman made Bill Clinton and Ronald Reagan look uncharismatic.

One week into the transition, I had to do the unthinkable—turn Maria down. It was a Tuesday morning. The sun was brilliant in a cloudless sky. Marcus insisted we walk three blocks to his favorite Cuban eatery. My mouth watered at the suggestion, and my stomach did somersaults as we entered and our noses were assaulted by warm spices and sizzling pork fat.

"God, I could come here every day," Marcus said as his eyes rolled back.

Maria chuckled and patted his arm. "Honey, you *do* come here most days."

I stood a step behind them and smiled at their affectionate familiarity. After twenty-some years of marriage, they still looked at each other like teenagers in love. It was impossible not to adore them; individually, and as a couple. As a campaign operative, I was trained to pay attention to my candidate, to watch for signs of instability or anything that might be perceived as a weakness our opponent could exploit. There were no skeletons in the Sanchezes' closet. I didn't think they even owned a closet—at least, not the kind where proverbial dead bodies were stored. They were truly good people.

"Joe, let's order before we get down to business, alright?" Marcus's serious tone caught me by surprise. We took our seats at a rickety wooden table in the corner of the restaurant. I gave Maria a quick glance, hoping for backup, but she just grinned and winked.

Something was definitely up.

Marcus ordered his usual pile of pulled pork, rice, and beans. Maria ordered iced tea, promising the nearly offended waitress she'd pick off her husband's plate. I started to order, but Marcus cut me off, rattling rapidly in Spanish to the waitress. I thought he said something about chicken, but that was the only word I picked up. For her part, the waitress beamed at his Spanish order, then gave me a grin and a brow raise.

Marcus's co-opted conspirator left the table, and he leaned forward. His voice was barely a whisper. "This is a difficult conversation for us, so I'll cut to the chase. I'm not going to offer you a position on my staff."

Wait, what? Had I heard that correctly? The statement stung like a whip crack. I'd done damn good work managing his campaign. Some in party circles openly boasted he wouldn't have won without me. How could he not want me on his team at all? Never mind the fact I hadn't *asked* for a role, but now that it was being pulled away, I wanted to know why.

Marcus's brows were knitted, his face scowled. I glanced at Maria and found she wore the same stoic expression—for about two seconds. My peek cracked her shell, and a wide, toothy grin split her face before she started giggling.

Marcus's head snapped to her, and he gave her a playful shove with his elbow.

"You're supposed to be serious—*mean* even. Remember?"

She giggled even louder. "I'm…trying…"

"Oh, screw it. Joe, we don't want you on our team. We want you leading it. Will you be my chief of staff?"

My jaw dropped. Diners at tables around us rose and applauded. For ten months, I'd been the conductor of the Sanchez orchestra. That day, the couple had organized a symphony of their own—*for me*.

I looked around the restaurant and realized we were surrounded by our campaign team and most ardent volunteers. In the few years I'd been working in politics, I'd seen operatives appointed to positions within administrations, but I'd never seen an appointment celebrated this way—certainly not at the hand of the candidate and his wife.

My throat tightened, and my eyes misted. Maria practically glowed.

Several minutes passed and the peanut gallery finally resumed their meals. Marcus quirked a brow. "You haven't given us an answer. Should we be worried? Do you have other plans?"

Maria reached over and put her hand on his, interlacing their fingers.

I lowered my head. "Marcus, Maria, I can't tell you how much you two mean to me. You're like family."

"But…" Marcus said.

"But…I'm a campaign operative, not a government official. You need a chief who already knows the players inside the government and council, someone who can smooth the road so your agenda actually passes and is implemented. I'd be starting from zero, learning as we go. That's not good enough, not for you or all you hope to accomplish. The people who elected you deserve better." I looked from Marcus to Maria. "I *want* to say yes, but I can't. Ten months ago, I promised to be your closest ally, to act in your interest—no matter what. As much as I hate telling you no, I can't keep that promise and do otherwise."

Silence hung over our table.

The waitress delivered our food. Still, no one spoke. Marcus and Maria stared into me. I fought every instinct to stand and run. Disappointing them hurt in ways I hadn't expected, but I knew in my gut it was the right answer.

Marcus finally nodded. "Joe, you *are* family now. You will always have a home, wherever we are," he said. "What will you do next?"

I tried to smile. "Get you through this transition. I'll have a shortlist of chief candidates for you tomorrow, then we can work on other positions. Once you're sworn in, I'll look for my next campaign."

Maria shook her head. "That sounds terrible, bouncing from one campaign to the next."

I shrugged. "It's what we do."

Two weeks later, Pete was offered a position within the new mayoral office as a policy adviser for healthcare. He'd spent the past several years working as a travel nurse with a regional healthcare company and was intimately familiar with the gaps in the healthcare system. I knew him as an irrepressible, horny gay who could light up any room with his rainbow flame, but he was also a serious medical professional with a keen mind built for strategic problem-solving.

He looked up from his half-eaten coffee cake muffin. "Why didn't you take the job with Marcus? You'd make a great chief. I could even get you one of those flowing headdresses with all the feathers. Wear that with nothing but a thong on Fire Island, I bet you'd be *really* popular."

"Nice. You made me a sexual object and offended indigenous people all in one sentence, Politicus Maximus," I said, laughing with my idiot friend.

"Politicus Maximus? I'm just a goddess of medicine. You're the political guru."

I rolled my eyes.

"Like I told Marcus, he needs someone with existing connections and experience within the city government, especially within the council and their staff. I don't know any of them."

He took a sip of coffee and cocked his head as if he didn't buy what I was selling.

"Stop it. You know me. If I had to stick with one thing for four years, I'd die. Besides, I want to work a statewide campaign now that I have a major local win under my belt."

"Before you jump back into working fourteen hours a day, you need to go out and let some hot guys get under that belt. You're wound too tight. A good lay will do you good—hell, it'll do *all* of us good for you to get some."

I smirked. I wasn't wound tight, was I? I was just professional and diligent.

"Nice try," I said. "Guys are a complication I don't need right now. Besides, all it would take is for someone to snap the wrong pic and post it online. I'd be untouchable for the fall campaign season. No dick is worth that risk."

His coffee thunked on the table a little harder than I thought was necessary.

"Whatever, Mary. I don't care if you spread your legs in public or sneak around in a back alley. You just need something shoved up that ass before I slap you back into the eighties."

My brows must've hit the ceiling because he started howling.

"That's right. Go get a good pre-campaign romp out of your system. Your staff will thank you—both of them, actually."

He tossed the last bite of muffin into his mouth and muffle-laughed all the way out the door, stopping once to turn and wiggle his fingers in a queeny wave. I tried not to grin, but couldn't help myself.

My eyes wandered around the Starbucks, searching for nothing in particular as I finished the last of my now-cool coffee. One older man sat pecking at his laptop at a table littered with plates. He'd been there for hours. Several college-age guys and girls were scattered at other tables. A tattooed and pierced barista leaned against the back wall, bored by the lack of work to be done. Then my gaze fell to the corner. The light from the single recessed bulb was dim. Two guys sat in overstuffed chairs, one with his leg draped over the other, their hands interlaced on the armrest. They were leaning so close their foreheads were almost touching.

One of the guys looked up, and I realized I'd been staring. My eyes dropped into my mug, and I tried to suppress the flush that crossed my cheeks. I wasn't even sure why I was embarrassed, but it felt like I'd intruded on an intimate moment. I risked another peek to find the guys again focused on each other. The guard dog who'd caught me now traced gentle fingers across the cheek of the other guy. Their smiles were so…I don't know…intent? That wasn't the right word. I wasn't sure I knew a right word for it. It wasn't a gaze I'd ever experienced.

I sighed and turned back to my coffee. What *was* I going to do next? The upcoming year was an off-cycle, with only the governor's office and a smattering of local seats up for grabs.

Our win for the governing job in the state's capital meant I would be a welcome addition to almost any campaign staff, but I really wanted to graduate to a statewide race. It was time I stepped up. I'd earned it.

My cell phone buzzed. "Hello?"

"Joe?" a husky female voice asked.

"This is Joe. Who is this?"

"Hi. Sorry, this is Tanya Mayer."

Tanya was the executive director of the state party. *Holy shit.* Why was the ED calling me?

"Uh, hi, Tanya," I fumbled.

She charged forward. "We want you on the gubernatorial campaign. Are you in?"

"Gubernatorial? Isn't the party supposed to wait for the primary to wrap before picking sides?"

She chuckled. "Joe, you're too seasoned to ask that kind of question. Now, can we count on you? The campaign needs an oppo research guy who can also give the candidate a waterboarding. From what I've seen in Nashville, you fit the bill."

Damn. Tanya had a reputation as a tough, no-nonsense party boss, but I'd never personally experienced it. There was no preamble, no introduction. She didn't even bother telling me who my candidate would be. She just went straight for the jugular.

I liked her a lot.

"If you're behind whoever this candidate is, I'm in," I said, mustering my campaign pro confidence.

"Great." She said it like she'd just ticked a task off her to-do list. "I know you're committed to the mayor until he takes the oath, but they'll want to brief you this week so you can start as soon as you're free. I'll have the campaign manager reach out and arrange the details."

Click.

My head spun and I stared down at my phone. She'd just hung up. Direct didn't begin to describe the woman.

I nearly popped a boner right there in Starbucks.

Before I could stand to return my mug to the counter, my phone rang again. Private number. That wasn't unusual in itself, especially considering the political people I dealt with, but it still sent an odd tingle down my spine.

"Hello?"

"Joe, Tanya just told me the good news. Welcome aboard." The smooth voice was familiar, but I couldn't quite place it. Shit, I hadn't even had time to stand up. These people moved at warp speed.

"Uh, thanks, I think. Who's this, and what am I on board with?"

The man laughed. It sounded painful, like something he didn't do often.

"Good one. This is Saul Peterson, campaign manager for the Reese campaign."

"Reese?"

"You've had your head in the Nashville scene too much. We've got to get you plugged in statewide." He spoke as though I was a five-year-old needing remedial kindergarten. "Reese is announcing for governor next week."

Well, *damn*. Congressman Snooty Nose *was* running for governor—and now I was on his team.

3

BUBBLY, SIR?

JOE

When he placed his hand on the Bible to be sworn in as Nashville's first Latino mayor, Maria's facade cracked, and a tear escaped. Marcus ignored the justice administering his oath and stared into her eyes as they committed themselves, together, to the people of the city. If I live to be a hundred, I might never see a more beautiful smile than the one they shared in that moment.

After a celebratory lunch, the new mayor and his wife began a full day of glad-handing and swearing in his newly appointed team. Technically, only the mayor was a sworn servant of the people, but Marcus loved the idea of giving his new staff the ceremony of taking a public oath. The press ate it up too.

I snuck out after the new chief of staff lowered her hand. This would be an administration of firsts for

Nashville. A Latino mayor and a female chief were just the start. I drove away filled with pride for all we'd accomplished—and for all Marcus and his team would accomplish.

It didn't take long for my mind to adjust to a new reality. I was on to the *next* campaign. I wasn't on the clock until sunrise the next morning, but I wanted to catch my new candidate giving a presentation at a fundraising event later that night, get a feel for his style and the campaign's level of speech writing. They'd hired me to do internal and opposition research, but I expected my role would evolve as the campaign moved forward. It always did. Besides, watching our candidate speak and interact with people was part of my research. I often learned more about one's personality—and personality flaws—by watching quietly from a darkened corner.

The event had originally been slated to take place in the home of one of our chief donors, a former ambassador to Luxemburg. Unfortunately, the good ambassador's wife had suffered a mild heart attack, and alternate arrangements with a local hotel were hastily thrown together. I walked into the miniature ballroom and was immediately impressed by the campaign's efficient conversion of the lifeless space into a festive, food- and wine-filled rally. Red, white, and blue bunting flapped with the perpetual blowing of the air-conditioning vents. Equally patriotic balloons bounced against each other as they dangled from ribbons tied to beams in the ceiling. Music alternated between John Mellencamp, Journey, and several other artists whose songs I could recite but whose names escaped me.

Men in suits and women in semi-formal gowns milled about.

"Glass of champagne?"

I nearly jumped out of my suit jacket at the sound of a tuxedoed thirtysomething carrying a silver tray of crystal glasses.

"No, thanks," I said with a smile. The server returned my grin, and I was sure he lingered a moment longer than was necessary. My hopes for a fun evening rose, though they were beginning to stray from any professional aim. Maybe Pete was right, and I needed to release some tension.

I watched Target One wade into the crowd and offer drinks to other attendees. He caught me staring and smiled.

A throat cleared behind me, and I nearly jumped for the second time in as many minutes.

"Joe, glad you could make it," came the rumbling bass of campaign manager Saul Peterson as I turned and looked down. Saul's salty hair barely reached my chest. Despite standing at five-foot-four, Saul was likely the largest person in the room—at least, the largest personality. He'd been managing campaigns for more than twenty years, with successful congressional, US Senate, and gubernatorial campaigns under his belt. He was respected within the national party, but was a legend at home in Tennessee. We were lucky to have him at the helm, though I was a little intimidated to be working directly for him.

"Thank you, sir. It'll be good to see the congressman in his natural habitat without him knowing I'm watching."

He chuckled. "Two things. First, never call me sir. I'm Saul. Second, I'm not sure this is David Reese's natural habitat."

"Sir? Uh, I mean, Saul?"

He rolled his eyes. "I like David. He's a good man, and he's served honorably, both in the navy and in Congress, but there's something I can't put my finger on that bothers me. No, that's not right. It *confounds* me—and I hate not knowing everything. Your job is to fill in the gaps, make me comfortable with the product we're selling."

"You're uncomfortable?"

Saul lowered his voice. I had to bend down to hear him. "No, I'm not. We have a good candidate. I just need to know what to expect, how we'll be hit. I can't prepare for an attack if I don't know what weapons the other side has." His eyes darted around, then met mine. "This isn't the place for this conversation. We'll talk more tomorrow. David's about to start speaking anyway. Get a drink. You're too stiff."

With that sage advice, Saul waddled toward the stage to handle whatever needed handling, leaving me with a spinning mind and a thirst for a guy offering champagne—I mean, for champagne. I wanted champagne.

I found a quiet spot to the side, midway back of the pack. A high-top table and two chairs offered a comfortable view of both the stage and assembled supporters. I wanted to watch my candidate while catching the attendees' reactions. I'd read after-action reports and seen videos of speeches, but there was nothing like catching in-person responses to political events. They had a certain feeling when done right. They had a *very* different feeling when things went wrong, something akin to an upset stomach mixed with a hangover headache.

As if timed with my butt hitting the stool, the booming voice of one of the local radio personalities sent a jolt through the crowd.

"Ladies and gentlemen, grab that last glass and gather 'round. Our guest of honor will begin in two minutes."

The music switched from upbeat classic rock to

grand orchestral pieces swathed in Americana. White spotlights aimed at the stage flickered, then switched to red and blue. Staffers who had previously manned the sign-in table began handing out small Tennessee flags. The whole place suddenly looked as though Tennessee's founding fathers had descended from Rocky Top and vomited all over the assembled flock.

The electricity racing through the crowd was immediate and palpable. Even the most bored-looking attendees and small groups huddling in back scooted for a better viewing location.

I chuckled into my drink. Frenzies were fun.

These were old tricks, but they worked every time, especially when the crowd was packed full of the most faithful of our flock.

"Ladies and gentlemen, please give a warm welcome to the next governor of the great state of Tennessee, David Reese."

And just like that, the sizzling reached the wick's end, and the crowd erupted.

Congressman David Reese, his hair perfectly coiffed and smile immaculate, bounded onto the stage with both hands high in waves far too grand for the intimate setting. It looked more like he was waving to a packed house of Titans fans in the Coliseum than a few hundred half-buzzed donors. I'd have to talk with his speech coach about that.

"Thank you, everyone," David said in a faux attempt to quell the cheering.

I had to stop my eyes from rolling. Every candidate loved the stage, but this bastard *craved* approval. How had I let myself get drafted to play on his team?

"It's time to bring common sense back to Tennessee!"

Every speech started with that line, though I'm not sure half the country could define what common sense meant anymore. It was our job to define it for them.

The crowd recited the last few words with him, punctuated by fierce mini-flag waving.

"Our leaders have forgotten why they were elected. From the look of things, they forgot why they ran for office in the first place..."

I stopped listening and scanned the crowd. There wasn't a person here who hadn't heard these words at least once, yet they hung on them as a parched man might lock onto a dribble of water being poured down his throat. One woman near the front caught my eye. Her eyes were wide and roamed up and down David's long torso. If he'd been a steak, she would've already devoured half of him. She was probably imagining him naked, with her tongue—

Dammit.

The mental image of David Reese naked flashed into my head. I shook it free. Starting tomorrow, I'd have to spend far too much time with him to have that picture streaking through my mind. Besides, who drooled over an arrogant prick? He might've been hot, but I had to maintain *some* standards. At least the server from earlier had champagne to go with his dimples.

I forced my attention back to the crowd.

I was a pro, but the sight both thrilled and sickened me. It was my job to win hearts and minds, but it always surprised me how easily some hearts were won. Minds tended to be harder nuts to crack. Luckily for political pros, voters rarely used their brains when choosing their favorite candidate. Base voters on either team pressed whatever color button their party dictated. Those in the middle tended to sway with whichever candidate made them *feel* good—or *less bad* in some races. My job— our campaign's job—was to package our guy or gal in the most trustworthy and likable way possible.

David's package gave us a leg up.

Just like that, I was seeing him naked again.

I stood and walked to the back of the room.

Twenty minutes later, David wrapped his speech with a few lines asking for donations. He ended with the oldest line in politics.

"Money is the mother's milk of politics, and this baby's hungry!" He patted his belly to a roar of laughter and applause, then waved through another chorus of orchestral Americana before exiting the stage.

"What did you think of our boy?"

I turned to find Saul again.

"He did well. A little grandstand-y, but we can adjust that. From what I've seen, he's good on stage and one-on-one." I nodded toward where David was shaking hands with a nerdy man in spectacles. I couldn't stop myself from offering a play-by-play. "His eye contact is strong, and he doesn't use a dominant handshake, even though that guy offered him a submissive, upturned palm. He forced the guy into a neutral shake to give him a sense of security and equality. Nice. See there? Watch the man's posture as they talk. He has to look up at David, but even with the height difference, David's deferring to him as he speaks."

I turned back to see both of Saul's brows raised.

"What?"

"You're *good*, aren't you?"

I shrugged, embarrassed by his praise. "I pay attention to details, that's all."

He grunted. "What did you think about the speech?"

"The speech was fine. Same ole shit. His delivery

and connection make it work. Crowd loves him—especially the blonde in the second row."

Saul nearly spat his whiskey. "Martha? Yeah, she's at every event. Spreads her wallet nearly as much as she'd spread her legs if he'd let her."

I raised a brow. "He hasn't?"

Saul glanced at me sideways. "Not a chance. He knows I'd personally cut off the offending body part if he went there. Martha's a wealthy donor. She's also slept with half our congressional delegation. But more than that, she's that woman in the church we tell a rumor if we want it spread to the four corners of the earth. She's a social network unto herself."

Interesting.

"So, you're sure—"

"Yes, I'm sure." There was a finality in Saul's tone that tickled the back of my mind. I started to ask about it, but he cut me off with a whisper. "Forget that Martha's a *terrible* match. David's wife died a few years ago. He was a wreck; still is, some days. He hasn't been on one date since, won't even consider it."

I nodded and made a mental note to add that to the growing list of topics to cover with our candidate.

4

GRILLED MEAT

JOE

I arrived at the Reese for Governor campaign office around seven thirty. More than a few butterflies battered my jittery stomach. I'd worked on eight campaigns, two as the campaign manager, but this was my first statewide race.

The front desk sat unoccupied, so I followed the sound of rapidly clicking computer keys into the main space where I pulled up short. The place was enormous. Rows of cubicles separated by short, movable walls filled a stadium-sized room. Long, empty card tables and folding chairs lined the walls to either side. The tabletop before every third seat held a shiny new telephone. I guessed those tables would soon buzz with activity as swarms of volunteers stuffed envelopes, stuck stamps, or did whatever else the campaign might need in the coming months.

I wandered down the center aisle and tried to process the scale of this effort. A prim woman in black horn-rimmed glasses looked up, and the pecking sound that had echoed throughout the room halted. She grinned and stood.

"Big, isn't it?"

I nodded absently.

"You must be Joe. I'm Carla, Saul's personal assistant. Well, yours too, I suppose."

"Nice to meet you." I stepped forward and shook her hand, unable to mask the wonder in my voice. "I thought Marcus's campaign was big, but we could fit four of our offices into this space."

"You guys ran a great race. Nashville's a tough place to win." She scooted backward into her seat. "Just remember, this campaign has *five* Nashvilles, plus all the rural spaces in between. We'll have more paid staff than you had volunteers, and that's just here in HQ. Our field offices will have even more."

My head spun. "When you put it that way, it really is incredible. I would say we're playing at a different level, but it feels like a totally different sport."

A snort sounded behind me.

"Different sport is an understatement." Saul put a hand on my elbow. "You'll adjust—just don't believe a word that woman says. She likes to spread lies, especially about me."

Carla laughed and waved a hand. "Saul? Was that a hint of humor? You'd better stop before Joe starts to think you actually have a heart."

She motioned for me to lean down so she could whisper conspiratorially, "Don't be fooled by Saul's crusty exterior. He's a softie."

"Enough plotting, you two. Joe, grab coffee and settle into the conference room over there. Kitchen is through the back door to the right." He pointed to a row of doors at the end of the floor. "It's the middle door, the closed one. I'll bring David in shortly."

I nodded, mouthed "thank you" to Carla, then strode down the last of the football field into the conference room.

At precisely eight o'clock, the conference room door opened. I sat sipping coffee. Saul wore a serious expression but was positively cheerful compared to the man who entered after him.

Congressman David Reese strode in—no, stalked in—like a leopard sneaking up on his prey. Maybe that was my paranoia and dislike of his perpetual arrogance talking, but it's how it looked. I rose and got my first close-up look at our candidate: six-foot-three of muscular tastiness in a light blue dress shirt—a slightly different shade of light blue this time, more sky than cyan —with rolled-up sleeves. The man obviously knew what suited him and he worked it at every opportunity.

I scanned him like he was paper in a copier. Damn, he might've been an ass, but he was a *hot* ass.

Protocol dictated I wait to be addressed. Reese sat and made me wait several heartbeats before offering a plastic politician's smile.

"David Reese. You must be Joe," he said, as if we didn't both know who we were and why we were there.

Let the games begin.

"Yes, sir. It's nice to finally meet you, Congressman," I said. "Thank you for doing the intro of Marcus on election night. He and Maria appreciated your public support."

His brows rose. "You arranged that?"

I nodded.

There was a slight pause as he and Saul exchanged a glance. "Thanks for that. Nashville's tough, and that put me on stage with a winner before our announcement. It was well played."

I hadn't done it for him, but I let him believe whatever he liked. Lord, did politicians always think everything was about *them*?

"Enough introductions. Joe's first task is research," Saul said as we took our seats.

"Okay," Reese said. "Why am I here then?"

I swear Saul's eyes glittered. "Oh, David, he starts with research on *you*. We need to know all the shit the other side will throw at us, and I've been working campaigns long enough to know you haven't been completely honest with me."

He held up his hands to stave off Reese's protest. "You might not have intentionally hidden anything, but everyone forgets. Joe's going to help you remember so we're prepared for any attack. You've won three congressional races. I'm sure you've been through this before."

Reese's eyes never left mine. It felt like a proctological exam of the retinae. After ten, maybe twenty seconds, I surrendered to discomfort and looked down.

"No offense, Joe, but I don't know *you*. Want to know all my secrets? Everything that could sink me now and in the future? Why should I trust you with that information?"

Saul silenced me with a look before I could speak. His voice was stern and brooked no argument.

"David, Joe signed a notarized NDA. The lawyer who drew it up is the former attorney general. Joe understands that we'll sue him into the eighteenth century if he violates it. Isn't that right, Joe?"

I nodded nervously.

"Good. No more nonsense. David, your calendar

is clear all day. Please don't leave before Joe's satisfied."

My jaw nearly dropped. Saul talked to the congressman like he was—

The door slammed behind him, leaving Reese glaring at me while I fought to pry my eyes from my hands. The only sound in the room was his fingers strumming against the tabletop.

"Have you decided there's nothing to find? Or are my secrets written on the back of your hands?"

God, I hated snarky bastards.

I sucked in a breath to steady my nerves.

Most candidates hated "the treatment," so I always started with the easiest topics to make them relax. For David, the low-hanging fruit was his voting record in Congress. He'd been a moderately loyal party man, voting more than seventy percent with the leadership. He'd strayed from the herd when bills conflicted with local agricultural concerns. Interestingly, he'd also parted with the party on a few key social issues. Tennesseans loved it when their guy stood up to the party, especially if the issue involved farms or farmers. The state's politics were generally divided more along rural versus urban rather than party lines. Reese's defiance of national politics in defense of local issues was viewed by most as a positive, but his social stances could be a problem.

We took a break after two hours, then resumed. Personal items now topped the agenda. I started with his years at Dartmouth. He was a hellion, a baseball player who liked to party. If he hadn't been a nationally ranked pitcher, he likely would've been expelled on more than one occasion.

This was where the fun began.

"Yes, I fucking inhaled," he said.

I tried not to grin. "Did you also sniff, snort, or shoot up?"

He winced. If his eyes could shoot lasers, I would've been smoldering. He was pissed, and didn't answer. That *was* an answer.

"Sir?"

"I heard you, dammit." He pushed himself back from the table and rose. "Yes, I did *all* those things. The entire team did, but that was a long time ago. I was a kid."

I made more notes, giving him time to elaborate.

He didn't.

"A kid? Old enough to vote and go to war. That won't sell, especially in this state."

I felt his glare as I continued writing without looking up. Pissing him off was fun.

"And since?"

His voice was a whip crack. "Since what?"

"Have you used recreational drugs since college?"

"Yes…but not recently…"

I tapped my pen against the table. "How *not recently?*"

"Are you sure you're not some kind of cop?"

"I'm *your* cop, sir." I gave him a tight smile. "Please answer the question. When did you last use recreational drugs?"

He walked around behind his chair, gripped its back in both hands, and leaned over. "Two weeks ago."

"What the fuck" slipped out before I realized I'd said it.

His brows practically slammed together.

"Sorry, sir. It's just…I wasn't expecting *that*." I took a breath and scribbled frantically. He eyed my paper from across the table as I underlined and circled something in angry, bold ink.

"Let's set drugs aside for the moment. Please understand, we'll need to know everything before this is over. Every gram, drop, needle—whatever. If you have *anything* in your possession that wasn't prescribed by a doctor or purchased in a pharmacy, I'll want to personally watch you flush it."

He shouted something, but I held up a hand. "It's me or *Saul*. Your pick."

His fire flickered out, then he nodded in surrender.

I made more notes.

Turning to a positive topic, I asked him to walk me through his service as a Navy SEAL. He'd spent ten years in uniform and was well decorated. Unfortunately, many of the questions I asked involved classified answers to which I wasn't entitled. Saul would bring in someone else to handle those queries.

We took another break, this time an hour for lunch. Reese was in a better mood when we resumed around two o'clock.

Time to go for the jugular.

"Are you gay?"

His eyes widened; the first betrayal of his mask I'd seen that day.

I waited.

He remained silent. His eyes found the back of his hands incredibly interesting.

"Sir?"

"I heard you." His eyes rose, fire in them now. Something had registered, but he was hiding it. I made a note on my pad. "Of course not. Why would you ask me something like that?"

"Because your primary opponent is already spreading rumors. I can only imagine what we'll face in the general—assuming we get there." I watched his reaction. He didn't flinch. "Several of your teammates from college are making the media rounds telling some interesting stories, including vivid details of a birthmark and…um…a sizable member. They're quite specific describing the way it curves. *Pitching* jokes are already running through the press pool."

He still didn't say anything, but his smug mask was slipping.

"Let's see. What else? You're forty-two, single, without children, and are considered handsome." I'd practiced how to word that last bit. He didn't need to know *I* considered him handsome.

He grunted and glared, so I pressed on.

"Fine. I'll continue." I pretended to check my notes. "No one has seen you on a date in years, not even the tabloids in DC—the same tabloids spreading the rumors. When you aren't being chauffeured, you drive a BMW Z4 with the top down. You showed up at the last Presidential Inauguration alone and attended the balls that evening without a plus-one. *No one* does that, especially not a sitting congressman. Your clothing is stylish, hair is always perfect, nails manicured—even your brows are plucked. Should I keep going?"

"My *Z4?* What's gay about that?"

I chuckled. "That's the spirit, Congressman. If you don't know it's gay, it can't be, right?"

"How dare—"

"How dare I what, sir? Talk to you like this? Ask about your sexuality? Insinuate you're a drug addict or a deviant? Or both?" I was feeling it now. "Which one? Which question am I *daring*, sir?"

His glare was now a full-on glower. I imagined cartoon steam puffing out of his reddened ears. The thought almost made me grin.

"I *dare,* sir, because it's what *you* hired me to do. I *dare* because I'm a professional, and I want to win. I want *you* to win." I sucked in a breath and lowered my voice to bring the temperature down. "Congressman, I'm *nothing* like what you'll face soon. You've won three congressional races, and that's impressive, but this is the next level. Our opponents are coming with both barrels loaded. Hell, they've been firing shots at you for a year in anticipation that you might run. Imagine the live fire you're going to take over the next ten months. My job is to make sure you're ready, to make sure *we're* ready."

The conference room shrank as silence hung in the air.

"No," he said, his eyes now riveted to mine.

"No, what?"

"No, I'm not gay."

I watched him for any sign he was quibbling, but his pupils didn't shift or twitch. I looked down and scribbled a note.

"Have you dated anyone in the past four years?"

His head drooped, then shook. It was like watching the air whoosh out of a pierced balloon.

"No."

"Why not?"

"Because…I…*I just haven't*." He snapped, suddenly animated again.

There were secrets tucked away. I could feel them just out of reach.

"Sir?"

"My wife died, alright?" His voice broke, and he deflated again. "Molly—"

I bit the end of my pen.

His voice lowered. "We were driving home from a Nationals game. It was our date night, the first one in too long." His smile was genuine as he recalled a happier time. "She ate funnel cake and got powdered sugar on her nose. We went to meet a couple of the players in the locker room, and one of them had to wipe it off with his towel. I doubled over laughing at her angry face. The player cracked up when he realized I'd let her walk in with a dusty nose."

I set my pen down and sat back.

"Molly…She usually drove, but not *that* night. She'd had too much to drink. We both had, but…"

He put his head in his hands.

"Sir? This is important."

"I know it's *fucking* important," he snapped, then

threw himself back in his chair and ran his hands through his no-longer-perfectly-coiffed hair. Wetness stained his cheek.

"Congressman, I'm sorry."

Another moment stretched.

He finally spoke. "David."

"Sir?"

"If you're the priest I have to confess *everything* to, the least you can do is call me by my name." He looked up, and a small boy stared back at me. "Please, call me David."

5

———

TEACHER'S NOTES

DAVID

First, he accused me of being *gay*, then he dredged up the worst, most painful experience of my life. This Joe guy they'd hired was on my last nerve, and I wanted to punch something.

I wanted to punch *him*.

"Sir, thank you, but I think I should stick to calling you Congressman."

My brows knitted. I'd tossed him a bone and he threw it back. What the hell?

I crossed my arms and nodded, bracing myself for the next round. I wasn't sure which was more unnerving: Joe's constant scribbling on that damn pad or his penetrating blue eyes that felt like Sauron's flaming eye above the tower, constantly seeking, never satisfied.

"How long were you married?"

The question snapped me out of my *Lord of the Rings* moment.

"Uh, three years. When she…When the accident happened, we'd just celebrated our third anniversary."

"I'm so sorry, sir."

Joe's voice carried tenderness, the first hint of something other than a constable's loathing of his suspect. I chanced another look. He was staring, but not like before.

"Why don't we take a break? Would you like some water or coffee?" he asked.

"Coffee would be great. Thanks." I nodded and watched him leave the conference room.

I stood and stretched. We'd been sitting for hours, and my back and butt were falling asleep. As I walked around the table to get the blood flowing, I realized Joe had left his pad. Neat script and tightly ordered bullets revealed much about my interrogator. One line jumped off the page. He'd circled it and drawn a bold question mark to its side. The mark had overdrawn lines like he'd traced it a few times as he mulled it over.

Gay. Denied. Didn't respond to college rumors. Something feels off?

Shit. I'd hoped we wouldn't revisit *that* conversation after I'd told him about the accident. Most people moved on when they learned my wife had died.

The door handle rattled, so I darted back to my seat.

Joe pushed the door open with his butt, then wheeled around with two steaming mugs.

"Black with one Splenda, I believe." He handed me the blue mug with the US House seal embossed in gold.

I smiled. "You know how I take my coffee too?"

He grinned for the first time that day. "Just doin' my job, ma'am…uh…sorry, I mean, sir. Just an expression."

I laughed. "It's okay, Joe. I *do* have a sense of humor. You can't believe everything people say about me."

Joe's smile widened. He cocked his head and paused before setting his mug down. "Ready to get back to it?"

I took a sip and nodded, raising my mug in salute. "Fire at will."

BY SIX O'CLOCK, I WAS EXHAUSTED. JOE LOOKED LIKE he was just warming up.

He surprised me by calling a halt. "Why don't we stop here? That'll give me time to review my notes and start the oppo research." Joe flipped the pages of his legal pad so the blank first page masked any handwriting below, then set his pen in the exact center of the page.

I chuckled at his precision. "I like the idea of you focusing your angry glare at someone else for a while. My eyes were starting to cross, and my stomach's been growling for an hour."

Joe grinned. "I heard the rumbles."

His eyes lit up when he grinned. That made me smile.

"Are you hungry? We could grab something better than the rubber sandwich Saul put on my desk hours ago."

Joe's mouth opened, then closed, then opened again.

"What?" I asked with a chuckle. "Is there some ethics rule about a campaign interrogator not eating with his target…I mean, candidate?"

He coughed a tight laugh. He'd been making me squirm all day, and it was fun to turn the tables a bit—though I wasn't sure why getting something to eat made him uncomfortable.

"Uh, sure. That'd be great," he said.

I stood and turned toward the door. "I'll ask Saul and the other senior staff if they want to join. They never stop working. I have to make up excuses to get them to eat most days."

Joe's expression was odd, a mix of confusion and something else…disappointment? Nah, that had to be the exhaustion and hunger talking. He was just surprised by his victim inviting him to dinner.

To my surprise, Saul had already taken the senior staff to dinner.

"Looks like it's just us. Thai okay?" I asked.

Joe switched his pad and pen from his right hand to his left, then leaned against one of the metal school-teacher desks. "Uh, sure."

I chuckled again at his discomfort. A few curls of his jet-black hair flopped across his forehead as he scrutinized some spot on the floor. "What's with the schoolgirl blush? Never had dinner with a member of Congress before?" I opened the front door. "Come on. It's a nice night out. Let's walk."

Tormenting my torturer was fun.

6

NICE SPRING ROLL, SIR

JOE

I followed the congressman out of the campaign office, unsure if my mouth and brain were still on good terms. Neither seemed willing to raise the logical objection to this ill-fated excursion.

What the hell am I doing? I thought. *This guy's my candidate, and I barely like talking to him at work. There's no reason I should be following him like a lost puppy. Fuck, his suit pants are tight.*

I shook my head and tried to stop looking at David's delicious butt.

He glanced back with a smirk. The jerk was toying with me. He might not be gay, but he knew I was—and he knew he was hot.

He turned and continued walking. My eyes drank in his lofty frame and his graceful, athletic gait.

Rounded shoulders swaggered either with confidence or arrogance, I wasn't sure which. It's a fine line.

What was I thinking? It *was* arrogance. He was arrogant, dammit.

Then it hit me. He was paying me back for the grilling I'd given him today, nothing more. Flirting with me was his way of dangling the perfect morsel before a starving man just to watch him drool.

Shit, I was drooling. I wiped my mouth.

We reached the restaurant a blessed moment later, and David opened the door, then did the last thing I expected—he held it for me. I nearly stumbled.

"After you, good sir," he said with a faux *Bridgerton* bow.

I shuffled through, and my attention snapped to a woman in a red-and-gold *chakkri*.

"Welcome." She smiled broadly, then glanced up as David appeared just behind me. I could feel his presence. My knees threatened to buckle.

My inner monologue screamed. *What's happening here? I don't even like this guy. In fact, I very actively dislike him. Oh, and he's my boss, my freakin' candidate. I should pretend to be sick, or have some campaign-related emergency. Yeah, that could work.*

"Uh…yes…two," I stammered.

David leaned in. His warm breath breezed past my ear. "Don't eat out much, do you?"

"Huh?" I said, stepping forward while turning my head back.

He chuckled. "Nothing."

I nearly jumped at the pressure of David's hand on my lower back, urging me to follow the woman.

The asshole was enjoying this.

Our hostess led us to a booth with tall wooden backs. They were covered in plush maroon cushions and carved into intricate landscapes. The artistry was stunning, but the effect of the high wooden frames offered privacy.

Great. Privacy with Congressman Smirky Ass. Just what I wanted.

"Ever eaten here before?" David asked.

I grabbed the menu and pretended to read it. "No."

"It's one of my favorites," he said. "Best Thai food in the city."

As if on cue, the kitchen door swung open, and an ancient man and woman raced toward our table. Each was elegantly dressed in traditional Thai clothing similar to the hostess. When they reached us, the woman pressed her hands together and bowed toward David.

"David, it is so good to see you again. It has been too long." The woman's heavily accented words carried as much flavor as the menu promised.

David ignored the woman's formality. He bolted

out of his seat and wrapped her in a tight embrace. Her tiny frame vanished into his. A heartbeat later, David had pulled the man into the hug, and I could hear the woman giggling beneath the huddle.

I couldn't help but smile.

"I'm so sorry, *mae*," David said as he pulled back. At his use of the Thai term for mother, the woman reached up and cupped his cheek. "It's so good to see you both again."

The man gripped David's arm as any father would. "Welcome home. I hope you stay this time."

David grinned and craned his head toward me. "If this guy's any good, I'll move back to Nashville for at least the next four years, maybe eight. Who knows?"

I startled as three pairs of eyes turned toward me. The woman pressed her hands together and bowed as she'd done earlier toward David.

"If you keep this one home, you will be family too." Her toothy grin was infectious and warmed my heart.

"We'll do our best," was all I could think to say.

"Sit," the woman ordered, transforming into the formidable matriarch she clearly was. I grinned as she shoved David back into the booth. She snatched the menu from my hands and David's from the table, then shook a bony finger at the congressman. "No menus for you. You know that."

As quickly as they'd arrived, the owners vanished, leaving David grinning wistfully at the kitchen door and me trying to find something for my now fidgety fingers to do.

"They seem nice." I was as articulate as ever.

David's voice was a memory echoing off a mountain. "I was pretty lost after the navy. They wrapped me in their arms and became my second family."

The layers of emotion in his voice caught me off guard. There was even more depth in his gaze.

I'd reviewed a hundred hours of tape before our session that day. He was a pro, a politician who wore a mask melded to his face. Every smile was perfect, his teeth gleamed, his eyes were always warm and bright. Even when he feigned anger on the House floor over some policy or position, I could tell it was part of a choreographed routine.

The *real* David Reese was always well disguised.

So why was he letting the mask slip now? We didn't know each other, not really. He knew better than to trust anyone, that even his own campaign team could betray his trust or inadvertently damage his efforts with a careless word.

He knew better.

I couldn't help myself. "Your service was pretty intense?"

His eyes returned to the present and found mine. The mask slid back into place. "You could say that."

Before I could pry further, the owners returned with steaming bowls of fragrant soup and plates of dumplings. David's stomach roared. I looked up and chuckled.

He grinned and shrugged.

The old woman's eyes darted from David to me as an unreadable expression crossed her face. She carefully arranged the dishes before us, but her eyes continued searching. I wasn't sure what they sought, but heaven help whatever they found.

"You need to eat, David. You have lost weight."

He huffed as though exasperated by her clucking, but his smile widened and his eyes glittered. "Yes, *mae*. Though I don't think I need to eat all of Thailand in one night, do I?"

She laughed and swatted his shoulder. "You eat what I bring you. Clean your plate."

As she scooted toward the kitchen, the old man gave David a sympathetic grin, then leaned in and whispered, "Better do as she says or she'll just bring more."

David nodded at the sage advice, stifling another laugh. The old man didn't stifle his, chuckling to himself as he strode back toward the kitchen.

We talked a little about the campaign, comparing

notes on his wealthy opponent, but spent most of dinner bouncing between Nashville's NHL team, the Predators, and chatting about the upcoming release of the *Game of Thrones* prequel.

I didn't know why it surprised me so much that David did normal-people things like watching television, but it did. His whole demeanor shifted when our conversation turned to Starks and Lannisters, and especially Targaryens. The man *loved* his dragons.

I couldn't blame him. They were seriously cool.

As our hosts brought out the third course, small plates containing squares of spongy cakes and oddly shaped cookie things, our conversation took a turn.

"Did you grow up here?" David asked.

He chuckled at my blank stare.

"What? You get to rake me over the coals, but I can't ask about you?"

I relaxed my shoulders, suddenly aware how they had tensed.

"Uh, sure. And yes, I grew up here. Went to Lipscomb from first grade through college. Got out for good behavior."

He spat Thai tea across the white tablecloth. "Good behavior? I didn't know Lipscomb was a prison."

I shrugged. "It's not, but living on the same campus for sixteen years could feel like a sentence."

"I guess."

Damn, his eyes twinkled when he smiled. He really needed to go back to brooding, or—

"And your family lives here?"

I nodded. "My mom does. We lost my dad a few years back."

"I'm sorry," he said. His eyes softened around the edges, and I could tell he meant it.

"Thanks," was all I could think to say as I grabbed another cookie to distract myself from his gaze.

"You really miss him, don't you?"

I turned the cookie over in my fingers, buying time before looking up. His gaze hadn't strayed, and I struggled not to look down again.

My voice croaked out in a raspy whisper. "Yeah. He was the best man I've ever known, my best friend."

"How's your mom doing?" he asked.

"Uh, she's okay, I guess. She'd never admit it, but she's lonely. I try to call every day or two, and visit each week."

I told him about my dad's cancer and how it took his life within weeks of diagnosis. Its rapid progression from treatable to terminal had caught everyone by surprise. The Vanderbilt medical team was one of the best, but even doctors lost the good fight sometimes.

He listened, never interrupting. His presence radiated warmth and empathy. I felt the need to tell him more. Why was I sharing my most personal story with a man I detested?

Some candidates were terrible in person. Not David Reese. David's eyes and ability to reach into someone were among his greatest assets. When a voter shook his hand and looked into his eyes, the world faded away. He gripped them. People loved that feeling of intimacy, knowing he wasn't just listening to their words, but was really *hearing* them. It was one of the things we'd play up as he did the retail politicking thing across the state.

In that moment, I understood the power of his gaze in a new, personal way.

Did I still detest him? That unspoken question nipped at my mind as he lobbed his next query across the table.

"You're an only child?"

I nodded.

Something flashed across his face, and he chuckled.

"Are you going to eat that cookie or just crush it out of existence? Did it do something to offend you?"

I looked from his smirk to my hand and realized I'd pulverized the poor pastry. Pieces of cakey goodness lay scattered across my plate. Icing coated my fingers. I dropped the last remaining piece and licked the sugar clean, then used a napkin to finish the job.

When I looked up, David was still staring and grinning, but there was something else in his eyes.

"Uh, sorry. Guess talking about my dad—"

He reached across the table and rested his hand on my forearm.

"Joe, it's okay. Thank you for sharing. I know that couldn't have been easy for you."

A jolt shot up my arm, and I knew I should pull back. He was just being sympathetic, but it felt more…I don't know…*personal*.

I didn't move. I couldn't. His gaze lingered, pinning me to my seat. I looked down and stared at his hand.

"Hot tea?" The elderly woman's voice broke the tension. I freed my arm and pressed it into the safety of the booth's padded back.

Her eyes darted between us again. I thought I saw a brow twitch.

David didn't hesitate. "Tea would be wonderful. Thank you, *mae*. Dinner was delicious, as always."

She beamed, then turned to walk away. I caught a quick sideways glance from her as she passed.

"She likes you," David said.

I opened my mouth to speak, but the brain-to-mouth connection failed. Why would it matter if the owner of a restaurant liked me? Why would he say that?

My heart quickened.

"Tea for two," a familiar voice said as two cups and saucers landed carefully before us.

I grabbed my cup and pulled it to my lips as quickly as possible, burning my tongue. It took everything in me to keep from spitting the boiling liquid all over the table. David's mouth quirked upward, but he didn't say anything.

"Thanks for coming tonight," David said between thoughtful sips.

"Sure. Dinner was great."

He sat back. "I either dine with donors or influencers, which is all work, or I eat alone. Everyone thinks being a congressman is glamorous, and I suppose parts of it are, but it can be lonely too. Everybody has an agenda. It's almost impossible to have friends. It's even harder to just relax and talk."

He wasn't wrong there. I'd seen far too many candidates say things they thought were in confidence only to wake and read them in the headlines the next day. Such was the price for fame and power.

"You should still be careful," I said, donning my campaign pro hat again.

He gave me a half-smile. "Even with you?"

I considered him briefly, then nodded. "With me.

With your campaign manager. With your mother, with your priest. Congressman, you gave up the right to trust people when you took the oath."

He snorted and shook his head. "Back to Congressman. Got it. At least I was David for a couple hours."

I hadn't expected that and didn't know what to say. He stood, hugged the owners goodbye, then motioned to the door.

"Our next session is the day after tomorrow, right?"

I nodded. "I think so, yes."

"Good. I look forward to it."

He walked out the door and turned right. I watched him disappear down the street toward his apartment, staring into the empty distance long after he'd vanished. Then I shook my head and turned left to head back to the office where my car was parked.

This had been a really weird day.

7

FUNDRAISING
DAVID

At nine o'clock, I rounded my desk and sat, finding a two-inch stack of paper before me. I flipped the first few pages to find full-page descriptions of potential donors, including past contributions to candidates or the party, events they'd attended, even personal information about their spouses, families, professions, and hobbies. Some of the sheets included a photo. The only other item on the desk was a telephone. Saul was thorough—and subtle.

Okay, maybe he *wasn't* subtle.

I scanned the first prospect, grabbed the receiver, then sucked in a deep breath. I loved talking with voters, hearing their stories and sharing my plans, but fundraising was painful. It also happened to be the lifeblood of a campaign. The media claimed this race required a minimum of ten million dollars for a candidate to be competitive, far more to win. If we did poorly in raising money, there would be no shot in November.

So, I smiled and dialed.

As the third hour of dialing began, the door to my office rattled and Saul entered.

"That's what I like to see, my candidate with the phone glued to his head."

"Fuck off."

He feigned offense. "So touchy, Congressman. Can't have you caught abusing your staff."

I chuckled and hung the phone up. "My brain is turning to mush. These calls are brutal."

His lips pressed into a line, Saul's version of a broad smile. "But necessary. You won't win—"

"Without money. I know. Thank you, sensei."

He gave me a dramatic kowtow. "What's the scoreboard up to so far?"

I flipped through the pages of completed calls and did some quick mental math. "Seven or eight thousand."

"Not bad for a few hours on day one. You might have a future here."

I snorted and rolled my eyes. Saul had run each of my three campaigns for Congress and knew I was a skilled fundraiser. He just loved busting my chops.

"How'd it go yesterday?"

It took a second for me to switch gears and realize he was asking about Joe's all-day interrogation.

"I think it went okay…other than Joe thinking I'm the spawn of Satan. Shit, that guy is rough."

Saul actually laughed. It sounded pained. "Good. He's doing his job if you feel a little shitty."

"Awesome. You hire people to make me feel miserable. Remind me why I keep you around?"

He shrugged. "Because you like winning campaigns, and I'm the best. That Joe kid's damn good too. You see what he did with Sanchez? Nobody gave them half a shot at winning, but they ended up on top by a wide margin. You need to play nice, give him whatever he asks for."

Something about the way he phrased that made heat flare across my neck. What the hell?

"Get used to these calls too. I asked Carla to block two hours of every day for fundraising. Either she or I will prep your call sheets. The weeks prior to our major dinners, we'll switch your script from retail to whale hunting. If Governor Konte agrees to be your campaign chair, he can take some of that burden off your shoulders, but you'll still be our best asset. You know as well as anyone how the big fish want to hear directly from you." Before I could respond, Saul turned and gripped the doorknob. "I'll get out of your way, just wanted to check in. We can do a recap later."

"Aye, aye, captain."

When the door clicked, I dug through the top desk drawer and fished out a napkin to wipe my now-sweaty neck. The room was suddenly suffocating. Why had a simple reference to Joe sent my temperature soaring? Maybe he pissed me off more than I'd thought.

Dabbing complete, I tossed the wadded paper in the trash, sat back and stretched my arms above my head. An image of Joe sitting across the table in the Thai restaurant flashed into my mind. He was looking down in his awkward, shy way, and my hand was on his arm. Was that memory real? When had I done that?

The sweat soaked through my collar this time.

I stood and paced the room.

It had been years since I'd had thoughts about another man. Molly and I met shortly after I left the navy. All those thoughts and desires had been neatly tucked into my mental locker and hadn't resurfaced.

Until now.

When I was running for governor.

8

———

SAM

JOE

Friday rolled around. You know, the day normal people celebrated getting a couple days off work? Unfortunately, campaign teams were anything but normal. As spring approached, I knew days off would be precious. Entire weekends off would be impossible. Fridays would turn into pseudo-Wednesdays, just another midweek hump to get over.

I was sifting through corporate press releases featuring our primary opponent when my phone buzzed. The handsomely rugged face of Sam Prescott appeared behind the Answer or Ignore buttons. I met Sam a few years back at a house party of some mutual friends. His arms and chest bulged beneath a ratty T-shirt. Some of the other guys whispered about the mechanic who needed new clothes. I couldn't stop imagining how good that shirt would look on the floor. Three whiskeys later, Sam had me pinned against the wall of our friends' bathroom.

Yeah, he was one of those rough, up-against-the-wall kind of guys.

He called me three weeks later. He didn't want dinner. He wanted more wall time. So, I gave it to him. Well, he gave it to me—and the wall.

We continued our mindless meetups every four or five weeks for the next three years. I was working back-to-back campaigns, which left little time for dating or a social life. Sam offered me a welcome release and never asked for anything in return.

I was never sure why we hadn't been on a real date, or even had a conversation with more depth than your standard porn script. From the few interactions we'd had where one of us wasn't pounding the other, he'd been a solid guy, nice, likable, super-cute. I knew he was a mechanic but had no idea what he actually fixed. I think he told me one night as I was struggling with his buttons. My mind was not focused on vehicle parts.

"Hey you," I said with a grin.

"Hey yourself. It's been a minute."

"Actually, I believe it's been about a month. If your cycle is still intact, we're due."

He laughed so loud I had to hold the phone away from my ear.

"I believe there are women out there who might be offended by your comparison, good sir."

My grin widened. "Perhaps. Then again, maybe you need to teach me some manners."

He growled. "I like the way you think, but…I have a crazy idea."

"You don't want to play 'tap it in every room' again, do you? My ass still puckers just thinking about it."

"Maybe, but not before I buy you dinner."

My brain seized up. Dinner? Did Sam just ask me out?

"Still there?" he asked. "You know, we've been doing…whatever we've been doing…for a long time, and I still don't know anything about you. I mean, other than how to bend you over—"

"Oh god, stop." I rolled my eyes so hard I was sure he heard them.

"That's what you usually say right before—"

"Sam!" I couldn't stop grinning despite my head spinning at his invitation. "I thought you wanted to keep things simple, especially since my job consumes my every waking minute."

"Slow down, tiger. I'm talking dinner, not shopping for curtains. I'd just like to know the guy I'm banging semi-regularly."

Huh. Dinner.

"Why not?" I said. "How about that Italian place on fifth?"

"Italian? Before 'tap it in—'"

"Stop!" I barked a laugh. "You're impossible. And I can't wait for you to find that spot again."

"Now you're making me rethink dinner; I'd rather go straight for dessert."

"Hey, this was your idea, mister. Italian, seven o'clock, wear something frilly."

My burly mechanic laughed again. "Nothing but the pinkest chiffon for you, my dear."

"Let me get some work done so I can be on time. And Sam?"

"Yeah?"

"Thanks. It'll be good to see you again."

"You too."

As we hung up, I realized I'd never heard his voice sound so…I didn't know how it sounded. It was different. He was always interested, at least in what was in my pants. Now, he actually sounded interested in something more than sex. Huh.

SAM WAS STANDING OUTSIDE THE RESTAURANT WHEN I pulled up. He was turned away, one hand scratching the back of his stubbly head as he perused the glass-encased menu attached to the brick wall. He hadn't shown up in pink chiffon, opting for faded jeans instead. His butt gave me a vertical smile as I climbed out of my car.

"Hey," he said, turning and taking a step toward me. His tight white T-shirt revealed more nipple than fabric. I nearly stumbled on the curb. Had he always looked so damn hot? He was like a combination of the *Peaky Blinders* guy and Henry Cavill.

"Hope you're hungry," I said. "This place serves massive portions."

He patted the belly that wasn't there. "Always. I'm a growing boy."

"You're a grower, alright." I elbowed him.

He held the door for me.

It took a moment for the gesture to register, but I couldn't stop thinking about it as we were greeted by a woman in a starched white shirt and black bowtie.

I drank wine with dinner. He opted for bottled beer. Every time he took a swig, I saw the tinge of grease or oil under his nails. Something about that hint of honest, manual labor made my pants tighten.

"So, we've known each other for years, but I don't really know anything about you. Where are you from?" I asked.

He took a long pull on his beer, then leaned back, his eyes drifting. "Well, my family's from Wyoming.

That's where I grew up. Dad runs land, raising cattle and sheep. Most days when I was a kid were spent on horseback or herding with our pack of dogs."

"Brothers and sisters?"

He nodded. "Six. I'm the middle kid of seven."

"Holy shit, that's a lot of kids."

"Yeah. You might think being the middle kid was bad, but my sister was the center of attention. The six of us protected her—no, *hovered* over her is more like it." He grinned at some distant memory. "We tortured the hell out of her too. Poor thing never caught a break, but she gave as good as she took. I think she could whip any of us now."

"Cows and sheep? The farm must be big."

"It's a ranch, not a farm. You'd get dirty looks if you called it that back home." He chuckled. "It's nearly three thousand acres, a little above average."

"Wow. Sounds massive."

He shrugged. "I guess. It was just home back then."

"You didn't want to work the farm…I mean, ranch?"

"Nice catch—and hell no. That's hard damn work. I love working with my hands, but running land like that, especially with herds, takes everything out of you. Besides, I grew up isolated from anyone who wasn't family. When I got old enough, I knew I wanted to move somewhere with more people than sheep."

"So why go from ranching to a mechanic?"

He thought a moment. "When I was fifteen, maybe sixteen, one of our rovers broke down."

"Rovers?"

"Yeah—think dune buggy meets Jeep. With that much land, we had to get around to make sure the fences weren't damaged, chase predators away, that sort of thing. We used rovers for everything. They were the best part of the job, a lot of fun."

He took another pull on his bottle. "Anyway. Dad made me help him fix the thing. I had no idea what I was doing. He'd ask for a lug wrench and I'd hand it to him, like some nurse assisting with surgery. Most of the time, I gave him the wrong thing. He'd either laugh or grumble from under the rover. There was something about figuring out what was wrong and fixing it, making something work again, that drew me in. I don't know. It just felt good."

The server appeared with two towering tiramisus. I could barely eat another bite, but Sam dove into his. He waved an empty fork at me.

"You are a sneak, you know that, right?"

I raised a brow mid-chew.

"You asked me questions all night. I did all the talking. Time for you to share, mister."

I chewed a few more times, then swallowed. "Ask away. I'm easy."

"Well, I know *that*," he quipped. "How'd you get into working campaigns? Seems pretty dodgy."

"Dodgy. I like that. I guess it could look that way from the outside."

He held up a palm. "I didn't mean—"

"It's alright. When people hear 'politician,' their skin usually crawls. I get it."

He took another bite and waited for me to go on.

"I don't know. It's just something I've always been interested in. I'd tell you it's my way of helping make things better, making a difference, blah, blah, blah."

"It's not?"

"Well, sure. I want to put good people in office who can make a difference, but I don't know if that's what drew me to campaign work. It's hard to explain." Now it was my turn to sit back. "There's a rush. It's like being on a job interview for ten, maybe twelve months with the people. Then, on *one* day, they either hire us or they don't. The pressure is intense, and there's never enough time. Every day is a maddening race."

"Sounds painful."

I laughed. "It can be."

"So, other than the rush, why put yourself through it?"

"You know the new mayor?" I asked.

"Marcus something?"

I grinned. "*Sanchez*. Marcus Sanchez. I ran his campaign."

His brows rose at this.

"He and his wife are good people—*really* good people. He's one of those candidates somebody like me dreams of working for. The race was crazy, like it always is, but I knew I was helping put someone in office who would make a difference, someone who could make things better."

"Huh. Kind of like fixing a rover, making something work better."

"Not sure I'd put it that way, but sure, I guess."

"So, I get what campaigns are, but what do you actually do?"

I drained the last of my wine. "For Marcus, I was the head of his campaign, which means I did anything and everything. I'm working for David Reese now doing research."

"Research? What's there to research in a campaign?"

"The candidate, our opponent, the voters, the media, donors, trends, you name it. The candidate and our opponent are my focus though."

The blank stare told me he didn't get it.

"I research our candidate to make sure we're prepared for anything the other side might throw at us. Opposition research helps us decide what to throw at the other guy—or gal, in this race."

"So, you dig up dirt?"

I laughed. "Something like that. It's not nearly as cloak-and-dagger as it sounds. In this campaign, our first opponent is in the primary. Her name is Shirley Wayte, and she's been a state rep for fourteen years. That's a lot of votes in the State House. I'm digging through them to see what might be questionable to our base, times she voted against the party or skipped voting altogether, stuff like that."

"Huh. Sounds…interesting," he said in a bored tone.

"Research isn't my favorite thing in a campaign, but it's what they hired me for. In a month or so, they'll move me to something else, probably leading the GOTV effort."

"GOTV?"

"Sorry, I forget most people aren't political nerds like me. Get Out The Vote is what that stands for. It's all the effort we put into getting our people to actually show up on Election Day. In a statewide race, the GOTV effort will be huge, involving all the staff and thousands of volunteers. I hope they give me that. It's fun."

"Sounds like herding cattle without the dogs."

I raised my empty glass. "That's *exactly* what it is."

The check arrived and, as promised, Sam wouldn't let me open my wallet.

"So, want some real dessert now?" he asked in a low grumble as he slid cash into the check jacket.

"My apartment?"

"Meet you there."

SAM BEAT ME HOME AND WAS LEANING AGAINST MY apartment door when I arrived.

"About time. Thought I was going to have to find some other guy—"

I threw myself into his body and drove my tongue deep into his mouth. He was startled, but recovered, and strong hands pulled me tight against him. He felt warm and hard.

I fumbled with my keys, finally managing to unlock and open the door. With nothing holding us up anymore, we tumbled through and into a pile on the floor. Before the door clicked shut, he had my shirt off and was sucking my right nipple. I groaned. His teeth sent shock waves across my chest. His hands flew up, gripped my wrists, and held them above my head.

"I'm gonna tear you up tonight," he said, as he came up for breath.

My mind couldn't catch up; a mumble was all he got in return.

He ground his dick against mine, and I forgot what I was trying to say.

The warmth of his tongue left a trail across my chest and around the other nipple, before heading north to tickle my neck. He kissed the soft flesh above my collarbone, then pressed his teeth down and pulled it up gently. I didn't know why that sent sparks through my brain, but fireworks exploded behind my eyes.

One hand released a wrist and found its way into my hair, pulling my head back.

When the hardwood finally became uncomfortable, he gripped my shoulders and lifted me into a sitting position. His hands teased my back as they inched toward my butt.

"Pants off, now."

We'd always been aggressive, but this was new.

"Yes, sir."

"Good boy."

I unbuttoned my jeans and wriggled out of them. Underwear was for the weak, and my newly freed cock leapt out.

"Oh yeah. There's my friend." He dropped to his knees and took me down to my balls before I could get my jeans off my right foot. I tried to shake them free, but his mouth and tongue were sending shivers so fast I couldn't think, much less focus. I stumbled back, but he braced me, then leaned me against the back of the couch. My jeans finally slipped loose as he gripped my hips and pulled me into him over and over.

"Oh god. You…uh…Sam…you're gonna—"

"If you do, I'll just make you do it again."

"Oh fuck!"

He pulled back and watched me struggle to calm myself. I reached down for him, but he slapped my hand away.

"Oh no. You do what you're told tonight. Ask permission before you do anything."

"Yes, sir. I promise." My nod was more like a frantic shake. "May I remove your shirt?"

He cocked a brow. "May you remove my shirt, *what*?"

It took me a second to get the game, then I grinned. This was going to be a fun night.

"May I remove your shirt, *sir*?"

"Better. I'll have to punish you if you keep messing up though." He slapped my butt playfully.

"Now, go ahead with my shirt, but slowly."

I gripped the bottom of his shirt and dragged it upward as slowly as I could. His stomach was flat, a hint of two abs showing. His chest, though, was a work of art. A dragon's tail inked in black circled his right nipple, its hoard to guard. The scaled head glared down from the center of his chest. I leaned over to kiss the beast, but Sam pulled my head up with two fingers on my chin.

"Naughty boy. Nobody said you could do that. Time to pay the price."

He whipped his shirt over his head and tossed it across the room, then grabbed me, spun me around, and bent me over the back of the couch. A loud *slap* was followed by a lightning bolt of pain. I jumped and squealed in the least manly way possible. His hand rubbed the spot he'd slapped, easing the pain and somehow transforming it into passion.

He stepped back. There was a zipping sound, then the thud of jeans hitting the floor. Everything in me wanted to turn to watch the show, but I knew that wasn't allowed, and I was determined to be a good boy. I was dying to know what he had planned next.

What I hadn't expected was Sam's hands suddenly prying my ass cheeks apart and his tongue spearing into me.

"Oh shit," I called out.

His hands squeezed my ass, and his tongue pressed deeper, wiggling wildly, pulling me open with warmth and wetness. His stubble grated against my tender skin, sending a totally different sensation through me.

A moment later, his face retreated and one finger slipped inside. I nearly screamed at the shock wave as he found my prostate and teased. A moment later, the finger vanished, and I heard the pop of a bottle cap. The finger returned, now slippery, and a second joined in the probing.

When his other hand gripped my cock, I thought I might lose it. I was so damn hard.

My breathing quickened. I grunted with each press of his fingers. He curled them down so they hooked just inside, and my body spasmed.

Then he pulled out again, and the room stopped spinning.

I tried to breathe. Everything had happened so suddenly.

The sound of a plastic package ripping made my head turn, but before I could see anything, Sam pressed his body against mine and slipped inside. His cock was average, but damn, he knew what to do with it. Ever so slowly, he pressed himself deeper. Then, just as slowly, he pulled back. Then again. And again.

Then he *slammed* into me.

I yelled, as much in surprise as in pleasure—and a little pain. He jerked himself back and rammed me again.

Fire flared in my chest.

My toes curled.

I thought I might pass out—or come. I didn't care which.

"I'm gonna fuck you so hard tonight you're gonna feel me for a week."

"Aggghhh," was my reply.

His hands gripped my shoulders and he picked up the pace, driving deep into me with every powerful thrust. He pressed faster, drove harder, until the couch scooted forward. The groaning sound of heavy furniture became erotic.

I surrendered. He felt so damn good. Fuck.

He held himself inside me, and I thought he might've come, but his hands gripped my shoulders and he pulled me up and pressed my back into his strong chest. He wrapped his arms around me and squeezed us tighter together.

Then Sam, the rugged mechanic, gently kissed my neck as he held me.

My body trembled more at that touch than it had at his aggression.

I felt him tremble too.

He nuzzled my neck with his nose, and I heard

him make a cooing sound, like a contented cat. I laid my head against his shoulder and savored his embrace, nearly forgetting the pulsing cock still buried inside me.

"What do you want, Joe?" he whispered in my ear.

For the hundredth time that night, he'd caught me off guard.

"I thought I was supposed to follow orders tonight."

His chuckle brushed against my neck. "Good boy."

He pulled us apart and turned me around to face him. There was something in his eyes…something I'd never seen before.

"I want us to stop. Everything's been so perfect. I want to…Well, I want *more*. To leave wanting more."

He held my gaze for only a second before his eyes dropped awkwardly to his feet.

9

DINNER PARTY WITH PETE
JOE

Pete gripped my arm and spun me around before I could grip the door handle.

"How do I look? Is my hair okay? It was such a mess."

I put a finger to my chin as though assessing something incredibly serious. "Hmm. I think—"

"You think what?" His hands flew to his hips as his head cocked at an odd angle, like a zombie with a broken neck.

I chuckled. "You look great—*fabulous,* even."

"Don't scare me like that. This party is a big deal."

I nodded. "Twenty years. I can't even imagine."

"Yeah, that too."

Now it was my turn to furrow a brow.

"Yes, the anniversary is remarkable, but I'm more interested in the single men who might be there to help celebrate. Who knows what *we* might find around the cocktail bar?"

"You're impossible. Tonight's about the guys, remember?"

"Oh, honey, they don't call it a *cock-and-tail* bar for nothing. It's always about the guys, just not the old-fart married ones you're thinking about." He strummed his fingers across his lips, pretending to think. "Oh, wait, maybe you are thinking about the right ones. Based on your couch-bending experience last night, you know exactly what I'm talking about."

"Oh, shut it."

He grinned and elbowed me. "Come on, spill. What are you gonna do? Sounds like Sam might actually want to date."

"Yeah, that's what I'm afraid of."

"Stop! What are you talking about? He's sexy, has a job, and he's into you. Oh, and he knows how to throw you up against a wall when you need it. What more do you want?"

"I…I don't know. I mean, I like him fine. He is super-hot, and the sex is insane, but I just don't feel… whatever I'm supposed to feel. Does that make sense? Hell, I don't even know what I'm supposed to feel."

"It doesn't make you tingle when he calls?"

"Does my butt quivering count?"

"That's something," he spat through laughter. "But

seriously, you feel *nothing*? You don't think about him or miss him between romps?"

I thought a second. "Not really. I don't think about him at all unless he calls or I get crazy-horny. Is that normal after three years of hooking up?"

"Honey, there's no such thing as *normal* anymore. You do you, boo."

Unable to take any more of Pete's banter—and annoyed at my own inability to feel anything other than lust for Sam—I turned and opened the door.

A tall, painfully thin Black man in a silky white shirt with ruffles on the sleeves stood in the doorway. Jackson and Rod, two of our closest and longest-standing friends, were celebrating their twentieth anniversary with an intimate dinner party. I snorted when Pete called it "intimate," as they'd likely invited more than a hundred and would have twice that many show up. Tonight's festivities had been the talk of the gay town for months.

"Oh, child, you're *early*. That's a gay *crime*," Jackson said with his usual flourish. "Rod might shit himself if he knows you're here. Poor thing's been messing with what little hair he has left for twenty minutes."

Pete shoved past us both, giving Jack a peck on the cheek as he did, then bounded up the stairs. "I'm on it, Mama Jack."

"I'm not sure who I feel sorrier for, your hubby or Pete," I said.

Jackson grunted. "True enough—but if anybody can get my beautiful gaysian in order, it's Pete." He turned back and pulled me into a tight embrace. "Thank you for coming, precious."

"Of course we came. You're family. Both of you."

He pulled back and smoothed out the wrinkles in my shirt he'd just created. Mom mode was kicking into high gear. I braced myself.

"When are you boys finding men of your own? I know you're still young, but that gay biological clock ticks faster than the straight version. We can't have you turning into an old maid. You'll be thirty soon, dear. It's all downhill after that."

He grabbed my hand and pulled me toward the kitchen, where platters of food were neatly arranged and covered in plastic wrap.

"Let's get you a drink," he said. "There might be a few candidates for you tonight. You know how word spreads in this town—almost as wide as my legs on a good night."

He cackled as he dropped ice into a glass and couldn't see the look on my face. There were few things I hated more than being set up, but Jackson and my mom were the worst. Their idea of "attractive" involved any man with a job and full set of teeth—and the teeth were negotiable.

"I have *one* candidate to worry about right now, and he's running for governor. No time for dating. Sorry, Mama Jack."

"Pshaw," he said, taking my mom's exact word out of her mouth. "There's *always* time to find a good man." He handed me a vodka tonic.

Thunder rumbled from the stairs.

"He looks spectacular. Mulan the man. The Chinese Cary Grant." Pete was on fire.

Rod trailed behind him, turning several shades of red with each nickname.

I set my drink on the counter and grabbed Rod, lifting him off his feet.

"Papa, we've missed you," I said as I squeezed.

"Can you miss me a little less? I can't breathe," Rod said, squirming.

I laughed and let go.

Rod's boots clunked as he hit the ground. He stood a towering five-foot-two, but had the frame and muscles of a bodybuilder. Even in his forties, Rod's physique was the envy of every guy in the gym, *especially* the meatheads in the free-weight section.

None of that stopped us from teasing him incessantly about his height.

"Aww. Look what Joe dropped. A little dumpling. Isn't that cute?" Pete chimed on cue.

Jackson stifled a laugh.

"You know this is our special day, right? You're supposed to be *nice* to us," Rod shot back.

"Ooh, Joe, this cookie has a fortune," Pete said lyrically.

I spat my drink.

"Come here, hon. Let me look at you before the big bad gays hurt your feelings." Jackson gripped Rod's face with both hands and kissed him.

Pete and I released massive sighs in unison, like teenage girls mesmerized by their first romantic comedy.

After twenty years, those two could out-mush a Disney flick.

When they pulled apart, their eyes lingered, and they smiled fondly. Jackson's fingers traced down Rod's cheek lovingly as they parted.

"God, saccharine overload. I can't take this anymore. Hand me a platter and tell me where to put it," Pete said, shattering the perfect moment.

"I'll gladly tell you where you can shove it…I mean, put a platter. Over there, on the buffet." Jackson pointed to a platter filled with cut fruit. "Just spread the others around wherever you see table space. The gays won't eat much anyway. They'll be too worried about bloating before going out. You know they planned a special after-party just for tonight—using *us* as the theme?"

"What's the theme," Pete said, "chocolate-covered egg roll? Sounds gross when you say it out loud."

We laughed and went about our assigned tasks. Jackson and Rod vanished upstairs to finish whatever last-minute preparations needed prepping.

"So, you haven't told me anything about Congressman Hottie Pants," Pete said, handing me a platter of mini sandwiches.

I snorted. "There's not much to tell."

"What do you mean? He's hot. You're working under him—or want to *be* under him—same difference, right?"

"Oh no, there's a big difference—and I don't want to be under him—or near him most of the time. He's completely full of himself."

"Hand me that one." Pete pointed to a bowl of grapes. "He could be full of *you* if you let him."

"Stop! That's disgusting. He's a *total* dick."

"Still?" he asked.

"*Definitely*. I mean, most of the time." I hadn't really processed what I thought of Reese over the past few weeks, and saying it out loud was more challenging than I'd expected. "One minute he's the Teflon candidate, barely reachable through that pearly white smile and thick shell. Then, without warning, he shows a glimmer of humanity, like there's a decent guy lurking beneath the muck. Then *bam*, the shields go back up, and he's an ass again."

"Sounds like a fun challenge. You'll win him over."

"I'm not trying to win him over. I just need to figure him out so we can win this campaign. I don't know…I feel like he's hiding something…something under the surface, something big. I can feel it."

"I bet you'd like to feel his *something big*."

"Why do I talk to you? Please tell me." I tried to sound serious, but couldn't stop a smile.

"Because I'm fabulous, and you love me."

He gave me a playful peck on the cheek and flitted back into the kitchen.

10

CHILE
DAVID

I strode into the conference room at seven thirty to find Joe already seated and reviewing a stack of notes. Three yellow pads were spread before him, neatly scrawled notes filling every line and margin. I hoped those overfilled pages weren't a sign of how many questions I had to face.

"Good morning," I said, as I set my mug of steaming coffee on the table.

He mumbled his greeting, waved his pen in the air, then resumed scribbling without looking up.

I sat and watched him as he finished his preparation. He wore a light blue dress shirt, almost exactly like my own. His sleeves were rolled up—again, like mine.

Then I noticed how the shirt clung to his chest as he leaned back and stretched.

He looked up, and my eyes darted to the blank wall to my right.

"Something interesting?"

"Oh…no…uh…just thinking there should be art on that wall…or something."

When I looked back, one corner of Joe's mouth was turned upward.

I decided to plow forward. "So, inspector, where do we begin today?"

He glanced back at one pad, closed it, then turned to another, scanning the page before looking up. "Tell me about your military service. Nothing classified, just a general overview."

So much for small talk. I nodded and braced myself for the long day to come.

By lunchtime, we'd covered my years in uniform —at least, what I could tell him. We'd also spent time on my business, people who worked for me, and the few who'd been fired under less than favorable circumstances. Joe was keen on knowing everything about those situations, though they'd never come up in past campaigns.

Following a quick lunch break, Joe grabbed a pad and paced at the head of the table. The morning hadn't been contentious, so I settled comfortably into my chair and munched on a cookie, unconcerned by the growing scowl that spread to his forehead.

"Tell me about Scott Winthrop."

The cookie scattered across the tabletop.

"What?"

He glared across the table's length, pad in hand, pen at the ready. "Scott Winthrop. Yes. You served together," he said matter-of-factly.

"Uh, yeah, we did. Scott was a SEAL…*is* a SEAL. You never stop being a SEAL, you know?"

"Right." He tapped his pen on his pad. "So, Scott. He comes up in your early media coverage a few times, then vanishes when you run for a second, then third term. All I can tell from the clips is that he was discharged dishonorably, and that your signature was on an affidavit that helped get him kicked out. You seemed angry at the time."

I stared blankly ahead. "We were brothers. Our unit, I mean. We were family."

The air conditioner suddenly thundered in the background. Joe's tapping sounded like gunfire, the paper rattling became ocean waves.

"David?"

I looked up without seeing him.

"You still with me? Where'd you go?"

"Chile."

Joe hesitated, then sat. "What can you tell me about Chile?"

Joe

I SAT ACROSS FROM HIM AND WATCHED HIM CLOSELY. The moment I'd said the name Scott Winthrop, his whole demeanor changed. It was as if he'd drifted back in time and was struggling to find the present again. There were so many emotions passing through his eyes, I could barely keep up.

"We were sent down on a drug interdiction mission. I know that sounds strange for the SEALs, but drugs were at the heart of our mission. It doesn't matter who or what. I couldn't tell you anyway. By the time we got into position, our target was long gone. Nothing remained of the workers or the camp. They'd burned every hut and building to cinders. I can still smell the charred shells of huts as we picked our way through. There must've been fifteen or twenty buildings when the camp was fully operational."

"Is that a large camp? I don't have any experience with this sort of thing."

"Yeah, huge." He nodded absently. "The ones I'd seen before were only a few buildings, designed to be hard to spot and easy to move. A lot of them even dig underground tunnels and caverns to stay off our satellite photos or infrareds. This camp looked permanent —almost like a small settlement—which meant it was important to the owner. We might not have captured anyone, but we definitely disrupted things, at least for a time. We raised a glass that night to our small victory."

"You stayed there?"

"Not in the camp, no. We hiked back to our extraction site, miles away from the ruins. Choppers picked us up as the sun rose the next morning."

I sat back and pondered the scene. "Okay, that doesn't sound like a disaster. Mission was a bit of a bust, but not a terrible result. Why is Chile such a bad memory?"

David had almost come back to the present. My question kept him pinned in the past.

"We were holed up in a large house at the edge of a village, a CIA safe house. Most of the team was huddled around a tiny television, watching a soccer match, I think. There was more booze than soccer. I was back in the bedroom writing up an after-action report. Command had made it clear they'd want it first thing."

"Okay," I said, still unsure where this was headed.

"I was lying on my stomach on the bed in boxers, lost in my notes. I didn't even hear Scott come into the room. Next thing I knew, his weight tugged at the mattress as one of his hands trailed down my back. I remember jumping so hard my pen flew across the room. He scared the shit out of me."

I made a note and waited.

"Scott reached down again and put a hand on my chest. I pulled back and said, 'What the hell, Scott,' right as one of the other guys in the unit walked in. Scott pulled back, but not before the lightbulb flashed in that SEAL's mind. He was our holy roller. The idea of one of his brothers being gay sent him through the roof. He shouted so loud the others left the game to see what was going on, a few with weapons drawn. I thought he was going to attack Scott right there, but he didn't, just started cursing in German."

"German?"

"Yeah, he was German. That doesn't matter. Bottom line, this was back when guys were kicked out for being gay. I was the unit's leader, so that task fell to me when we got back home."

"You had Scott discharged?"

David's head fell. "Yeah. I had to see it through or my team might think…I mean…The guys saw that. What was I supposed to do?"

Just when I was starting to warm up to this guy, I learned what a coward he really was. My stomach turned. I focused on my job. "The look on your face tells me there's more here," I said flatly.

He looked up. The moisture in his eyes caught me by surprise.

"He killed himself a month later. A bullet to the head."

"Shit."

"Yeah."

Now it was my turn to stare at the table. I had no idea what to say. David spoke before I could form the next question.

"Scott was a great guy, the one you'd want to be stuck with when the shit hit. He was what a SEAL *should* be."

"Except for being gay, right?"

David's head snapped up. Fire blazed in his eyes. "That didn't fucking matter. He was a damn good SEAL."

"But it did matter in your report, right?"

David shoved himself back so hard his chair slammed against the wall and toppled over.

"Fuck you, asshole. You don't know *anything*," David raged. "Goddamn it. We saw more ugly shit in a few years than most people see in a lifetime. Scott was there, *always* there. He always had my back. Hell, he probably saved my life a dozen times over." He leaned across the table and stabbed his index finger at me. "He was a *good* man, and nobody's ever gonna say otherwise. You get me? Not a bad word about Scott. Ever."

It felt like I was staring into the eyes of an enraged lion that was deciding whether or not to attack. Everything in me wanted to bolt, but I couldn't move.

A moment later, David straightened, sucked in a few breaths, then ran both hands through his hair.

"I'm sorry. That was a difficult time—"

"David, it's alright." I tried to sound calm and reassuring.

"No, it's not alright. I fucking *killed* him. All he wanted was to be loved, and I drummed him out of the navy and killed him."

He threw himself back into his chair and the strong, impenetrable man melted before my eyes. He pressed forward on the table, his head resting on his folded arms. His shoulders shook as emotion overcame reason.

A moment passed, then two, then ten. Without thinking, I rose, knelt beside him and placed a hand on his shoulder. For another few moments, neither of us moved, then he looked up. His eyes were lined with red, and his cheeks were stained. I knew I should've stepped back, given him space, but I didn't.

Steel gray eyes locked onto mine, then his hand rose and traced my face with his fingers. I shivered.

He gave me the tiniest of smiles. When my brain caught up to whatever the hell was happening, I staggered back and practically fell over before slumping back into my chair.

"I'm sorry," David said. "I...I don't know. I...got lost for a moment."

His eyes still hadn't left me.

"Uh, I think we...um...maybe that's enough now. I have notes...and things...*campaign* things...We're good for today." I leapt up and darted out of the room, leaving my pads on the table and David's eyes staring at the back of the conference room door.

I RACE-WALKED OUT OF THE HEADQUARTERS, CAREFUL to avoid catching anyone's eye. The last thing I wanted was for someone inside our operation to know David had gotten under my skin.

I slammed my car door and leaned back into the comfort of the worn leather. What the hell just happened? Had I imagined an *intimate* moment? Had David...I mean, the congressman...just come on to me?

Surely not.

He was caught up in a memory, a bitter, sad memory. That was all. His hand was a reflex. *My* hand was a reflex, meant to offer comfort and support. Yeah, that's all that was. It *had* to be.

I glanced down at my watch. It was eleven o'clock in the morning. We had another five or six hours scheduled, and I knew Saul would kill me if I wasted our candidate's time. That was the cardinal sin of a campaign: wasting time. There were always more donations or yard signs or volunteers—but there was never more time. It was precious.

But how could I go back in there?

On a whim, I grabbed my cell and pressed the first speed dial in my directory.

"Hey, precious. How's the hot candidate? Is he diddling his staff yet?" an excessively perky voice chirped.

"Pete!" I stifled a laugh. "Stop that. I need…well…um—"

"Oh shit. He diddled *your* staff, didn't he?"

"No! Stop that. He's still an asshole. There's been *no* diddling." My head pressed against the cushioned rest. "But—"

"But? There's a but? I knew it!"

"Pete!" Why had I called him? This was a day filled with bad ideas. "Never mind. I just had a rough morning and wanted to hear a friendly voice."

"Mm-hmm. Mama Pete doesn't believe you, but I have to run. Mayorette Maria wants a lunch date, and you know I can't refuse the first lady of Nashville in her time of need—even if that need is only for fabulous company and chardonnay."

I chuckled. "Give her my best."

There was a pause. Pete's voice sobered. "You know you can talk to me about anything, right? Call me later. Okay, hon?"

"Yes, Mom. Thanks."

I grinned down at the phone as Pete's smiling photo vanished. There was no way I could tell him. Suspicion already wove through his effervescent voice. It wasn't that I didn't trust him, he could keep a secret. It was just…I wasn't sure *what* had happened. I was even less sure how I felt about it.

AROUND TWELVE THIRTY, MY FEET LED ME BACK INTO the office. Carla gave me a wave from across the still-empty room. I asked if she'd seen David, and she pointed a hitchhiker's thumb to the conference room.

I opened the door slowly and peered in. David stood looking out the window that comprised the back wall. The view was of a dumpster and three parking spaces, so I knew he was thinking rather than sightseeing.

My pulse quickened. I cleared my throat, and he turned.

"Oh, hey. You're back."

"Yeah. Just needed some air. It gets so stuffy back here."

His mouth turned upward. "The room or the company?"

Was he *joking* with me? Did he even know how to joke? He'd always seemed so stiff—until he wasn't. He'd relaxed at dinner, seemed almost human for an hour. Crap. We'd had dinner. My pulse kicked it up another notch.

I gave him a tight smile and shrugged, unsure if I trusted my brain to control my mouth.

He took his seat and folded his hands on the table. "What now? Did you get what you needed about Chile?"

His mask was firmly in place, as if the morning had never happened. How did he do that?

"Yeah. I think so. If I think of other questions, we can revisit." I opened my notepad and nodded. "Why don't we go back to your voting record? Five years in Congress racks up a lot of votes."

"Okay. Sure." He sounded unsure. "Um…should we…talk about what happened…you know, earlier?"

My pen slipped out of my hand as I looked up. I

didn't know what surprised me more, him stammering or wanting to talk about him caressing my cheek.

"David…*Congressman*—"

"Joe, I'm sorry. I don't know why I did that. It was incredibly unprofessional, and I apologize."

That wasn't how I thought that would go. In every version of this conversation my mind had crafted, he berated me for being gay or weak or something. He was nasty and curt, our working relationship forever frayed. My mind tended toward the half-full side of most equations.

Then there was one absent daydream that came unbidden—and unfiltered—where David locked the conference room door, then closed the gap in two strides before taking my face in his meaty palms and—

That daydream—I mean, nightmare—*had* to get out of my head.

Where had that come from? David might've let me see glimpses of himself, but he was still the same arrogant jerk I'd watched turn his nose up at our rally.

Oddly, no one else in the campaign seemed to think of him that way. I'd been listening for the usual watercooler talk that came with an unmanageable candidate. There hadn't been a single negative word so far. Not a peep. Even Saul, who had become more open with me than I'd expected at this early stage, talked about David like he was a long-lost brother.

Was he *really* that good with people? Did he cast some magic spell I didn't know about?

Why was I even having this debate? He was my boss and that was it. I mentally slapped myself back into reality and looked up into his questioning eyes.

"Um, okay. No problem. It was a difficult subject, and…well…you needed a friend. Simple as that." I shuffled my papers without looking at them. "So, back to votes?"

He eyed me a moment longer, then nodded. "Sure. Back to votes."

11

THE NEW GUY

DAVID

I t had been a long day, but my mind still raced, and my heart felt like elephants had trampled on it. A workout usually calmed my soul, so I decided to run for an hour—or ten.

I walked back to the apartment I was renting, tossed my candidate's uniform of slacks and blue dress shirt onto the bed, and changed into shorts and a Naval Academy T-shirt.

It took me three attempts to tie one sneaker.

I couldn't focus. Every time I closed my eyes, I saw Chile.

I hated the damned Selva Valdiviana. Locals called it the Valdivian Forest. It was Chile's southern-most rainforest and the home of several notorious drug lords, one of which was our target on the mission I'd told Joe about. When we first arrived in the jungle,

I remember thinking it was the most beautiful place on earth. There were plants and birds found nowhere else on the planet—and they were everywhere. Sure, it was a death trap waiting for any unsuspecting prey to offer itself in sacrifice, but it was also a stunning wilderness, an example of the splendor of untouched nature.

It was also where things heated up—before they went horribly wrong.

I finished tying my shoes, then shoved earbuds in my ears and cranked up some nineties dance music, the kind with the hard driving beat that would force my jog into overdrive. I wanted to punch something, but I *needed* to sweat, to get whatever this was out of my system.

Halfway around the block, my mind's eye replaced monkey vines and ferns with Scott Winthrop's face. I could see every curve and line as if I'd seen him yesterday. My pulse quickened as I gazed into his eyes.

Nine months prior to the Valdiviana mission, Scott had been assigned to my team. We hadn't been deployed in a while and spent most of our time training on remote beaches in California. Scott was green, fresh out of SEAL training, and we were his first assignment.

As I jogged past a Dunkin' Donuts, I noticed a guy

sitting at a counter staring out the window. He had Scott's jet-black hair.

I'd never seen hair so black, like it drank in all the light around it. And given the missions we would undertake, we didn't shave our heads like most in the military. Scott's messy mane flowed in whatever direction the wind blew—and most of the time, that meant it half-covered his face.

Hence, he earned the callsign Sheepdog.

The guys were relentless, especially with a newbie. Scott took it all in his stride.

No, that's not right. He ate it up. He took their teasing and banter for acceptance and offered himself as the team goat. He made more fun of himself than they made of him—and they loved him even more for it.

Add to all that, the bastard worked his ass off.

In all my time in uniform, I'd never met anyone who worked harder or gave himself so completely to his team. I didn't think the guy ever slept or took a break. If anyone struggled, he was there. If anyone was upset or frustrated, or their nerves were fraying, Scott was there, by their side, offering a kind word or shoulder or ear.

He was an incredible guy and an even better teammate—the kind you wanted by your side when bullets started flying—because you knew he'd do *whatever* it took, no matter what it cost him.

We became best friends almost immediately, and no one thought a thing about it, including me. We were just two SEALs on the same team who'd bonded through training and battle. It's what was *supposed* to happen to brothers in arms.

BY THE TIME I STAGGERED THROUGH MY APARTMENT door, it was dark outside. I'd jogged for nearly two hours. I was drenched in sweat, and my mind raced faster than it had before. The run was supposed to calm things, help me sort them out.

No such luck.

Worst of all, as soon as I'd shake myself free of painful memories, Joe's face would appear. Again and again, the sensation of my hand brushing lightly against his cheek sent shivers down my arms. I nearly ran into a light pole thinking about him, seeing his smile.

What the hell was happening to me?

I thought all these feelings had vanished—or been stowed away, at least. Molly had been the best thing to happen to me. I loved her with all my heart. When we were together, no one else existed.

So why, now that she'd been gone a few years, were feelings I thought were well buried suddenly rising to the surface? What was it about this Joe guy—the jerk who wanted to pick at every scab and dredge up every secret—why did he make me want—?

What *did* I want? Did I even know anymore?

Could a candidate for governor even entertain…? Of course not, my rational mind answered. *Especially* in Tennessee.

I tossed my dripping clothes on the floor and strode naked into the bathroom. The shower took forever to heat up, so I found myself leaning against the wall with a wandering mind and stiffening cock.

Joe had gotten into that head too, apparently.

Without thinking, I reached down and teased it with my fingertips. It hopped, sensitive and eager for action. Joe was suddenly there with me. I could feel him, smell his cheap cologne mixed with Dove soap. I gripped myself and gently stroked, imagining his hand was loving me, feeling my chest and—

Fuck.

My hand flew away, and I hopped into the shower, hoping the scalding water would wash away whatever had gotten into me.

12

THE STATE FAIR

JOE

The next weekend, campaign season began in earnest.

The annual State Fair, held at the Tennessee State Fairgrounds, heralded the true start of the battle for elected office. Whether a candidate sought to represent a rural county or urban center, they were expected to don jeans or coveralls and kiss the fatted pig, or in some cases, wrestle it.

As a sitting congressman and candidate for governor, David was one of the most high-profile politicians in attendance. That meant his opponent, Shirley Wayte, would also be there. Each would shake hands, kiss babies, and give a speech before a bored crowd who cared more about snow cones and cotton candy than anything they had to say.

But no one bucked tradition. Ever.

Saul insisted the senior team also attend. We'd hired a fundraising director to work alongside our fat-cat volunteer campaign chairman. We'd also acquired a volunteer coordinator. Each would be busy enlisting attendees and handing out flyers. My sole purpose was to check out our opposition, to see how their message and staff were received, and to compare notes when the candidates spoke.

We were expected to stay until the gates closed, making this a twelve-hour day. I'd likely have only one hour of useful work to do. Desperate to avoid mind-numbing boredom, I talked Pete into tagging along. When he showed up in coveralls, cowboy boots, and a straw hat, I wondered what I'd been drinking when I'd thought his presence was a good idea.

"I'm ready to have the best time *evah, sugah*," he said in the thickest Southern accent he could muster.

"If we win this campaign, I may have a state trooper shoot you. I just want you to have fair warning."

He pulled a straw out of his hat and chomped it. "Let 'em try. I'm hard to get, hon."

I groaned. This was going to be the longest day ever.

"Oh, look." He pointed across the park. "Isn't that *your man*...I mean, candidate?"

"Shush!" I snapped, then lowered to a whisper. "You can't even joke like that here. The press knows who I am and will have people everywhere listening for something juicy. With the rumors the Wayte camp is tossing around, your little quip could end up on the front page of the *Tennessean*."

"Alright, fine. I'm sorry," he said. "It's nice to work for someone already in office. I don't have to worry about every little thing anymore."

He was quiet a moment as I scanned our immediate area for spies.

"What rumors?" he leaned in and whispered.

"Huh?"

"You said Wayte was spreading rumors. What are you talking about? I've been kind of busy with mayoral stuff."

I grabbed his arm and pulled him to a shaded path that led to a fenced-off employee-only section.

"They're saying David's gay, or at least that he's had gay experiences. You know Tennessee, especially rural Tennessee. If they believe he even looked at a gay magazine, his campaign will die."

"Huh."

"Shit. I know that tone. What *huh*?"

"I don't know. He's kinda set my gaydar off a few times."

"What? Seriously? Did he do something? Hit on

someone? What did you see? Pete, this is important. I need to know."

"Easy." He raised a palm, his eyebrows peaked. Then he whispered, "I didn't see him *do* anything. It's just—"

"Just what?"

"I don't know. He's always so well put together. I mean, look at him over there." He motioned with his head, and I followed to see David shaking hands. His light blue shirt was crisp, and his jeans were pressed. Who pressed jeans? Yet another thing to fix. "Ignore the snooty look on his face, and just look at how he's dressed and all those muscles poking out when he moves. That fucking hair is *never* out of place. I officially hate him."

We watched for a moment, then he asked, "Does he pluck or are those natural? They *can't* be natural. I'll hate him more if they are."

I rolled my eyes. "He plucks. I've covered that one."

His eyes widened, then he nodded as if I'd just proved his point. He wagged his index finger at me. "It all starts with the brows. He'll be sucking dick in public before this is over. Mark my words."

"Fuck me. Why did I invite you?"

"Because I look *fabulous* in coveralls—and that's hard to pull off." He laughed. "Enough shop talk. You need to win me a giant dildo…I mean, stuffed dinosaur. I saw them at the ring toss thingy near the entrance. Come on."

I shook my head and chuckled as he dragged me from the safety of the shaded fence line. We passed a dozen yards from where David was glad-handing. He caught me watching and gave me a quick nod.

"Did he just smile at you?" Pete hissed in my ear.

"No, dummy, he acknowledged one of his staff passing by. It's polite. You read too many romance novels."

"Oh, I do love a good smut book. There's a new one about bears and otters mating in the wilderness. It's called *Rutting Season*. You should check it out."

I snorted again. "By the way, your gaydar hasn't worked since the nineties. It beeps at pretty much any dick, as long as it's attached to a mammal."

"Oooh. Mammal. I could get into a good grisly right now."

"What you need is a tranquilizer. Right in the butt cheek."

THE SUN WAS SETTING ON THE COOL SPRING DAY WHEN we finally made our way to the pavilion where vendors sold every kind of hamburger, hot dog, and fair delicacy imaginable. Pete was adventurous, trying everything he could get his hands on, but I drew the line at unidentifiable things deep fried then dipped in chocolate. By the time we located the stage where the politicians were gearing up, Pete was turning a pasty shade of green.

"Oh god, I think I'm going to throw up," he said, bracing himself on the back of a folding chair.

I chuckled. "Told ya political speeches were bad for your health. Oh, and the food here too."

He groaned and sat. "I can't believe you're making fun of my misery."

"Oh, sweet one, you'd be disappointed if I missed the free shots when you are too weak to fight back. We have standards, remember?"

"Fuck you and your standards. I want Tums. Stat."

"Yes, Nurse Jackie. Let me see if anyone has a med kit. Don't move."

He groaned again. I took that as agreement he'd sit still, then patted his shoulder and scanned the booths lining the pavilion walls until I found one with a giant red cross.

A few minutes later, I returned to find my patient where I'd left him.

"Holy shit, he does know how to behave. Call the press."

"Fuck you. Give me my meds."

"Is this your bedside manner?"

"I'm the patient, moron. Patients have no manners. Ask any nurse."

I chuckled and handed him the chewable tablets the medic had given me. "Down the hatch, and no more bellyaching."

"Oh god, stomach pain jokes. I may die."

"I'm not that lucky. You'll probably spew all over someone important and get caught on tape. I'll spend weeks cleaning up."

His laugh was pained. "Please don't make me laugh. That's the worst—and will make me…oh shit."

He hopped up from his seat with one hand over his mouth and darted toward a restroom door.

Shirley Wayte was on stage when he returned. I was sitting quietly, pad in my lap, pen tapping against it.

"That chocolate fried ring of death is *much* worse the second time."

"Shh," I hissed. "This is what I came to hear."

He harrumphed and settled into his seat, arms crossed. I glanced sideways and was relieved to see he looked less peaky than before.

"Did I miss anything?"

"Nah. Normal campaign trail BS. They'll refine her message over time as they identify hot issues. I'm more interested in how the crowd responds to her. How she handles herself."

"And?"

"She's a pro," I said. "Worse, she comes across as believable and empathetic."

"Crap. I hate it when a politician is real."

"Idiot." I chuckled. "She's our *opponent*. We want her to be hard to like—but, from what I've seen today, she knows how to grab a crowd and hold them, how to make them like her. Hell, *I'm* fighting the urge to like her."

"You can't like her. You already like David."

"Pete! Not *here*," I snapped, then lowered my tone. "Besides, I barely want to be in a room with him. I definitely *don't* like him."

"Mm-hmm."

I started to respond, but a booming voice called over the speakers, "Ladies and gentlemen, Congressman David Reese, candidate for governor."

The crowd offered polite applause. Their hands would be numb by the end of the night.

I sat up straighter.

"You're tapping faster. Something got you hot?" Pete whispered.

"Why don't you go eat something fried?"

"That's below the belt. Maybe a little above it, actually. But no, thank you. I'll stay right here and see how the Honorable Dreamy McDreamy does on stage."

I wanted to stab him with my pen, but the nickname was actually funny. Images of campaign signs with the golden arches flashed in my mind.

I needed therapy.

Just as we'd choreographed, the crowd laughed, then applauded. Our speech was well rehearsed and David's delivery was pitch-perfect, as usual.

Twelve minutes had passed as our guy waved his final farewell and left the stage.

"Well, how'd he do? Did the Russian judge screw him again? Or was that the Czech? I can never keep them straight."

"Have I told you how glad I am you're not working on this campaign?" I grinned and poked his leg with my pen. "He did fine. He always does fine."

"But?"

"But…there's no feeling. His words are right, and he says them well, but they aren't translating into emotions. The crowd gets it, they just don't *feel* it, and I have no idea how to make him less…plastic."

I made a few more notes while Pete wandered over to a stand selling purple iced somethings. He returned moments later and shoved a spoon in my face.

"Okay, this was worth everything today. Eat that."

The plane came in for a landing, so I didn't have much choice but to open up and swallow.

"Dear god, that's got *rum* in it!"

Pete grinned and thrust a full plastic cup at me. "Uh-huh. And mama got you one of your own."

I shoved my pen into the spiral of my notepad and grabbed the proffered treat. "Bless you. I may save you from the tranquilization after all."

"So, you never asked me what *I* thought of McDreamy's speech."

I cocked my head and fought off brain freeze. "Okay, what did you think?"

He leaned in and whispered, "I think he looked at you *three* times in a ten-minute speech."

I nearly spat purple. "You're kidding. We're halfway back in a crowded room. He probably couldn't even see me from up there."

"Oh, he could. The snow cone stand is by the stage. I could see you just fine, and I wasn't standing three feet off the ground to get a better view."

"Okay, fine, but that doesn't mean he looked at *me*. He scans the crowd when he speaks. That's speech one-oh-one."

"Oh, honey, no. He was looking at *you*. Your head was down when he did it twice. His eyes lingered like he was waiting for you to look up. He eventually moved on when you didn't."

I still hadn't told Pete about David caressing my face. I didn't even know where to start. Hell, I couldn't explain it to myself, much less to my judgey best friend. The idea of David seeking me out in the crowd at the State Fair was more than my brain could process. It *couldn't* be true.

"You're serious?"

He nodded and crossed his arms. "Mama knows these things. Trust me."

I wanted to argue, but couldn't think of anything to say. My mouth opened then—

"Joe, good, you're still here," a smooth voice said from behind us. My cup of purple, rummy deliciousness splattered across the floor as I fumbled to my feet.

"Uh, sir, sorry."

David laughed. His teeth practically glittered in the lighting, and his eyes crinkled slightly at the edges. I wobbled, catching myself on a chair back. Pete took a step forward and extended a hand.

"Congressman, I'm Pete Cabrea, Mayor Sanchez's medical adviser."

David took Pete's hand, and his smile shifted slightly. "Nice to meet you, Pete. So, you know Joe from the Sanchez campaign?"

"We go way back. He's my best friend."

David nodded. His smile didn't flinch, but his eyes twitched.

Then he turned back to me, and his eyes relaxed. "I'm glad you were here. What did you think?"

"You did well, sir. We'll go over my notes tomorrow, after I've reviewed them with Saul."

"Please stop calling me sir," he said, then turned to Pete. "This guy's killing me."

"Mm-hmm. I bet he is," Pete said.

I shot him a glare.

David's eyes danced between us.

"I'd better get going before Saul accuses me of wasting time. Nice to meet you, Pete." He turned and waded back into the crowd.

"Oh. My. God. He's *so* into you." Pete clapped the tips of his fingers together and hopped like a rainbow-colored pogo stick—in overalls and cowboy boots.

"Will you calm down. *There are people everywhere.*"

"That wasn't a denial. You saw it. Tell me you saw it."

Pete wasn't going to stop, so I elbow-dragged him out of the pavilion and toward the park's exit.

"I didn't see *anything*. That was David asking the campaign staffer responsible for assessing his speech how he did. Period."

Pete pulled his arm free and stopped, planting it on

his hip. "He can't hide that thing with his eyes and the corner of his mouth."

"What are you talking about?"

"His smile changed when he went from me to you—and don't give me some bullshit about how he knows you and doesn't know me. It was more than that." He leaned in and whispered, "He's into you."

"I'm back to having you sedated. They're going to empty the whole gun…or magazine…or whatever it is they empty out of a tranquilizer."

Pete locked arms with me and skipped, laughing all the way to the parking lot.

13

YES, YOU

JOE

Weeks passed in a blur. Our first internal poll showed us up by seven points. David was the darling of the Tennessee media, and morale among our staff and volunteers was high. For a campaign only a few months out of the crib, the enthusiasm was palpable.

The campaign office was a beehive of activity in anticipation of our first of three bus tours across the state. Lamar Alexander had set the standard decades earlier, traipsing across Tennessee in his red-and-black flannel shirts. It didn't matter whether he visited cities or farms, the people ate it up. He won two terms without breaking a sweat, and went on to serve as Tennessee's senior senator in Washington.

We hoped to replicate his success—sans flannel.

The schedule for this first tour called for stops in

Clarksville at Fort Campbell, a visit to Murfreesboro and Knoxville, where David would whip up mobs of students at Middle Tennessee and the University of Tennessee. The bus would pause near Dollywood (more for fun than campaigning) on its way to the final destination in the southeastern corner of the state, Chattanooga.

It would be a week of exhausting travel, fundraising dinners, and speeches. David would kiss hands and shake babies—well, vice versa anyway. Before the week ended, David would deliver the same stump speech a dozen times.

The whole thing sounded grueling, and I was looking forward to an easy week back in the office focused on my research of our opponent.

"So, you ready for this?" Saul asked, opening my door without a knock.

I looked up from a stack of news clippings. "Uh, ready for what?"

"The tour. What else?"

"Yeah, I guess. You guys should kill it. David's good on stage."

He cocked his head. "You're coming too, right? The road time will let you finish your interviews with him. I want the candidate report next week so we can work on a rapid response strategy with the communications team."

"Oh shit. I, uh—"

"You didn't think the whole team was going on the road and leaving you here, did you?" He laughed in the way an evil cartoon character does right before tying the damsel to the tracks.

"Well, no, of course not," I said. There was no other answer, dammit. "I still need to go home and pack though. Mind if I leave a little early?"

"No, that's fine. We leave at five o'clock. Make sure you're here by four."

In typical Saul fashion, he didn't wait for a reply, just wheeled about and slammed the door behind him.

14

FORT CAMPBELL

JOE

O nly an hour after the bus left Nashville, soldiers with mirrors examined the underside of our bus. The gates to Fort Campbell stood proud and alert.

"First time on a base?"

I turned, surprised to find David settling into the empty seat beside me. There were only five of us on a full-sized bus. Saul had come to visit with thoughts or questions a few times, but I hadn't expected David to saddle up beside me. He'd remained cloistered in his private compartment in the back until now.

"No, but first time on Campbell."

"They're all the same."

I nodded like I understood. I didn't.

"Some have newer paint, are in better states of repair, that sort of thing, but they're all packed with soldiers or sailors or whatever branch happens to be there at the time. Testosterone and patriotism flow almost as freely as alcohol."

I turned back to watch as the bus was motioned forward.

"Thanks for coming on the trip," he said. "I heard you weren't planning on it until Saul…you know…did what Saul does."

"Yeah. That's a good way to put it."

He reached across me and pointed out the window. "That's the main headquarters building. We'll take a tour, shake hands with the brass, get a few photos."

His arm brushed my chest. A hint of cologne and musk from being trapped on a bus for hours drifted into my nose. The combination was heady. I tried to look where he pointed, but my eyes rebelled and turned to meet his. Our faces were inches apart. He exhaled at the same time I sucked in a breath, and his air flowed into me. I couldn't stop a shiver. He lingered, then sat back, still not breaking eye contact.

"Uh, okay. Sounds good. Um, I need to hit the bathroom before we, um…de-bus…get off…I mean, park—whatever you call it."

He chuckled at my distress. "They have restrooms in the HQ."

"I really need to go *now*. Excuse me."

I scooted past him, desperately trying to avoid

noticing how our bodies pressed against each other, then fled the full length of the bus to the restroom in back. When the click of the door latch sounded, I closed the toilet lid, sat, and stared at the No Smoking sign without really seeing it. What the hell was happening? Why was my heart pounding and blood raging like a wild river? David was making my head spin in ways I'd never felt before.

Fucking David Reese.

Why *him*? I'd rather Saul…no, scratch that. But I'd definitely rather it not be David making all this heat flare in my body.

I couldn't possibly like the asshole.

No, that wasn't it. Maybe it was just some chemical reaction when a hot, muscled, toned guy with perfect teeth and wavy hair—and a devilish grin—brushed against me—

Oh god, take that image out of my head please.

I turned to the tiny sink and splashed water on my face. It didn't help.

I was burning up inside. Images of David leaning over, pressing against me, flared to life. I wanted to feel his breath, taste it, breathe it with him. I wanted to rip that perfectly pressed blue shirt off him and hurl it across the room. I wanted—

A knock at the door made me jump so hard I banged my head on the back wall.

"Hey, Joe, we're unloading. Hurry up. HQ tour in five." Saul's voice was the slap I needed to refocus.

Bless you, Saul.

A SHARPLY DRESSED SOLDIER OPENED THE DOOR TO the headquarters building. David nodded, then strode in. Our team of four trailed behind like a disorderly pack of puppies. We were greeted by more men and stars than I had ever seen in one room. There was a three-star general, several two-stars, a handful of one-stars, and a whole flock of birds. It was an impressive gathering of military brass, and I briefly wondered who was holding the shield while we stole their attention.

"Congressman." The three-star stepped forward and extended a weathered palm. "Welcome to Campbell. We don't normally let squids on base, but I'll make an exception for a member of Appropriations."

In that moment, I remembered two things. First, David was a SEAL, which meant he was in the navy. The general was duty-bound to invoke interservice rivalry and give him shit. Second, David was still a serving member of Congress and sat on the all-important Appropriations Committee. The whole of government—which meant the entire military—was funded through that committee. The generals didn't exactly kowtow to David, but they were certainly respectful, to the point of deferential.

I stood back and watched as David walked the line of green-suited leaders and realized the power of his position—and the weight it must be on his shoulders. His title declared him one of the four hundred thirty-five members of the lower chamber, but his true role as an important leader of the nation hadn't sunk in until that moment.

Had I worked in campaigns so long that I'd become numb to the offices to which I was helping elect candidates? Had I forgotten their import, their authority, their *impact* on the lives of ordinary people? Something in that moment made me wonder if David's arrogance wasn't some sort of defense mechanism, a shield against the arrows that were fired at one in his position. Everyone wanted something from a congressman, but how much more sought-after was someone with the power of the purse?

Every officeholder *chose* to run. They raised their hand. No one made them take the oath. No one forced David to run. There was no sympathy for those who volunteered to stick their feet into the fire. And yet, watching the interaction with some of the army's most senior officers, I felt an odd sympathy for him. I didn't know him well, but I could see the wall he erected as he switched from speaking with us behind closed doors to facing those in the public arena. He donned armor and lowered his visor, like any knight headed toward battle. He also withdrew a part of himself. I supposed it was a self-preservation thing, but the isolation that came with such a public position was striking—always surrounded, yet always alone.

I'd never really thought about it until that moment.

David made some funny remark I couldn't hear, and all the men in uniform laughed. It looked like *practiced* laughter, the kind one gives a superior whether or not their remark was funny. His comment felt scripted, and so did their mechanical mirth.

David looked back and caught me staring. Something flitted across his face, some emotion I didn't recognize or understand. He wiped it away quickly and gave me his most manicured smile. I curled my lips and nodded in reply.

When all the greetings were finished, Three-Star led us into a large stadium-theater-style room with massive monitors on one wall. Images from satellites and drones were displayed on most, though a few showed Google maps of various regions. At the bottom of each screen flashed the word UNCLASSI-FIED in bold yellow lettering.

"This is the ops center," Three-Star said in his best tour guide voice. "Every active operation is monitored from here. When an op goes hot, most screens switch to views of that particular action. As you can see, we've displayed unclassified video today. If there is anything specific or classified you'd like to discuss, Congressman, we can go to the SCIF. It's fully equipped with video and teleconferencing."

"I'm just a guy running for governor today, General. Thank you though."

The military men chuckled again. They reminded me of a bad chorus who knew enough to sing but not which notes. It felt *so* forced.

We strode into another stadium-style room, this one used for training and briefings. Two generals and one colonel presented various topics. David leaned forward most of the time, peppering them with questions throughout. I fought to stay awake.

Three-Star finally reclaimed the stage and concluded our tour. I shuffled in my seat, eager to get the photo op finished and hit the road again.

David surprised us all by asking, "General, would you mind having someone show us to the medical facility? I'll keep all the cameras outside. It'll just be me going in."

Three-Star nodded, and I caught a hint of a smile cross his stony, weathered face. "Yes, sir. Of course." He turned to a man to his right. "Colonel, see to it."

Hands were shaken, and our contingent followed

the colonel out of the headquarters, across a parade ground, and into a massive metal building with red-and-white Red Cross flags flapping in the breeze.

As we approached the entrance, David turned and held up a hand. "This one's just me. I'll be twenty or thirty minutes. Why don't you all go back to the bus and relax?"

Saul and the others turned as one. For some reason, I found myself pinned in place, watching David. His eyes drifted, watching our people disperse, then landed on me. He cocked his head and paused—that thing I'd seen earlier, that unidentifiable emotion that had crossed his face, crossed it again. I still didn't know what it was.

"Joe, would you come with me, please?" he asked formally.

"Uh, okay…sure."

We followed the colonel through double doors and the world transformed from barracks and parade grounds into a typical hospital, complete with sterile white walls and tiled floors. Outside, we were the odd folks out of uniform. Inside, lab coats and scrubs replaced fatigues and dress greens. A bleachy aroma made my nose wrinkle.

"Where to, sir?" the colonel asked.

"B wing," David said without hesitation.

He gave me a quick glance over his shoulder, then

turned to follow the colonel. There was something…*meaningful* in that glance. It looked like a cross between sad memories and physical pain. I was suddenly aware of every doctor, nurse, and patient as we marched down halls and through swinging doors. There was a feeling to the place, beyond what I'd felt in other hospitals—a sense of purpose. Maybe I was projecting my own subconscious image of all things military. I don't know.

We finally rounded a corner and stopped at a pair of solid-looking double doors. The colonel swiped his badge and the doors swung open. I'm not sure what I expected, but the twentysomething with tightly cropped hair on crutches wasn't it. The boy—man, I supposed—was missing one leg and wore an eye patch. His head snapped toward us as we entered.

The colonel continued past with a simple nod, but David didn't. From two strides back, I watched him approach and grip the guy's shoulders with both hands. The patient seemed startled at first, but relaxed as soon as David spoke. I couldn't hear what he said to him, but the guy beamed, and his posture straightened. The guy looked at David, then noticed me standing a few strides away. It was as if David had breathed light into his previously hollowed eyes.

With a final squeeze of the man's shoulders, David nodded, released him, then turned to follow the colonel. There were nurses on duty behind a large counter, but none moved to bar our path. We entered the first patient room we encountered. The door swung shut behind me, and I stood with my back against it. It felt like I was intruding on some private moment, so I kept my distance. The colonel found a corner opposite and became a statue as David approached a bedridden patient.

The woman's face was burned—so much so that I doubt she was recognizable to anyone but friends or family. I cringed, but David strode forward.

"Hi, Susan. I'm David."

The woman's eyes flitted toward him, blank and unreadable, then that same light flickered to life and she smiled weakly.

"Congressman—"

"Stop that. I'm either David or Captain. You pick." He gripped her hand and sat on the side of the bed.

They spoke for only a few minutes before David looked up at the colonel and nodded. The weight that pressed so heavily inside that room had lifted, if only slightly.

"Thank you, David," the woman called out. "You're my first visitor, you know."

I opened the door and stepped out quickly, not trusting my heart to stay where it belonged. From the safety of the hallway, I heard David say, "Susan, you get better. We need you. You hear me?"

"Yes, sir. I will."

AN HOUR LATER, WE'D VISITED EVERY ROOM ON THE floor. David walked in knowing the name and condition of each patient, some whose injuries were likely beyond repair. I fought back tears, but by some gift of magic, David lifted the spirits of each patient. It was a small gesture in the grand scheme of their recovery, but I knew it was somehow important, though I didn't fully understand why.

"Colonel," David said to our guide as we exited the hospital.

"Sir?"

"Joe, you hear this too." His voice brooked no argument. This was a naval officer issuing an order. "What you just saw and heard didn't happen. Understand? It's off the books, and no one—especially the media—is to hear about it. Joe, not a word to Saul or the team."

"Yes, sir," the colonel barked, and I found myself mimicking him.

David insisted the colonel return to his duties, that we would find our way across the base and onto our bus without a guide. Neither of us spoke as we walked. Our strides were as slow and deliberate as the images coursing through my mind. I'd attended more campaign rallies and events than I could count, but I'd never been moved as I had that day.

"What did you think?" David asked halfway across the parade ground.

I opened my mouth and tried to put my emotions into words, but nothing came out.

He huffed a sigh of recognition. "I know. It gets me too. Every time."

"Every time?" I asked.

"Yeah. I do a lot of base tours. You know, the whole member of Congress gig?" He smiled weakly. "I make a point to visit the equivalent of the B ward you saw today each time we do a tour. I don't know if it helps…I hope it does, at least a little."

He choked out that last part. I glanced over and watched him look away and wipe his cheek. And then I tripped on a curb and sprawled face down in front of two guys in fatigues.

"Sir!" they said in unison as they dove to help me up.

"Are you alright?" a soldier with cropped black hair and crystal blue eyes asked as he gripped my arm. I nearly swooned. He was stunning—and dammit, he smiled.

I forgot my English. "Yeah…uh…I guess...well...I'm just a klutz."

I glanced down at his hand still lingering on my arm. My heart played a drum solo as our eyes locked again. Why was this guy still staring at me? And why wasn't I getting up? Like an idiot, I was still splayed out on the ground gaping at my uniformed savior. His other hand reached down and gripped mine to pull me up. I felt a tingle at his touch. His eyes said he did too.

David's stern voice shattered the moment. "I've got this, soldier."

Before I could think, the sexy soldier's hands were replaced by David's as he shouldered the man out of the way. The smell of tangy aftershave filled my nostrils as he leaned closer. The soldier's touch had made me tingle, but David's hands were a warm, cozy blanket wrapping around me and pulling tight. I tried to shake that sensation, but his hands, still firm in their grip, squeezed my arms comfortingly. His brows were creased, his gaze intense, and I swear there was fire in them—not the fire of passion or lust, but of something more primal —*protective*.

He looked up at the soldiers, and his well-practiced stage voice returned. "Go scale a wall or shoot something, boys."

"Yes, sir!" they barked in unison and trotted off.

"You okay? Let me look," David said, hovering, his grip unwavering.

"I'm okay. Just a couple scrapes."

He helped me to my feet, one hand on my arm, the other bracing my elbow.

I brushed my palms free of the road rash that was forming and peeked up to see David's concern was now a smug grin.

"You're really graceful, you know that?"

I rolled my eyes. "If you weren't my boss—"

He chuckled. "Go ahead. I'm an asshole. I know you're thinking it."

I startled. Had he heard me call him that? Had he overheard Pete and I at the fair? "No…*sir*…I wouldn't—"

"Yes, you would—and I *am* an asshole. But I'm a *funny* asshole, and that's what counts."

I tried not to smile, but dammit…

15

ROAD TRIP

JOE

Textbooks taught us that Tennessee was divided into three grand divisions: middle, east, and west. The geography and topography were almost as different as the people who lived in each region. This concept was so engrained in Tennessee culture that it was represented on our flag by three white stars at its center.

Our next stop was a tour and student address at the University of Tennessee in Knoxville, home of the Tennessee Volunteers. Knoxville sat perched in the upper right corner, only a few dozen miles from the border of several other states.

Eastern Tennessee, despite the high college-age population, was the conservative base of the state where the Republican elephant charged through yards almost as often as dogs and cats. David represented a more purple district in Middle Tennessee, and teetered dangerously on the line of a moderate to liberal member of the GOP. He touted conservative fiscal policies, and his military service made him an instant hero, but his social agenda strayed from the herd. All this made our trip to base land interesting—and critical if we stood any chance in the primary against a hardcore conservative opponent. The students at UT were our best hope of cracking the shell of the East Tennessee egg.

I spent most of the three-hour drive reviewing notes and scribbling suggestions for Saul. He'd asked me to look over David's planned speeches, and I relished the opportunity to get my hands dirty on something other than oppo research. Saul was beginning to let me into the inner circle, and I didn't want to let him down.

"Hey! I like that line."

My red pen had just bled through a not-so-witty quip in the UT speech. The double seat shook as David flopped down beside me, leaned over, and pointed to the offending revision.

I gave him my best 'you can't be serious' glare.

"So *not* funny, Congressman."

"Come on, college students love me." He shifted in his seat, leaning so our shoulders pressed together even when he wasn't pointing at the page.

I sucked in a breath without meaning to. That familiar tang drifted up my nose and into my mouth—damn, I *tasted* him. I shook my head free and tapped the page with my pen, adding unintended dots to the strikethrough.

"That line's dead. You can appeal to Caesar, if you like."

He grinned. "And here I thought I wore the crown."

I chuckled. "Have you met Saul?"

"Fair point."

I continued flipping pages and making notes.

He didn't move. His shoulder didn't move. His breath and aftershave—and presence—continued to press against me, into me. I lost the war of distraction and set my pen down.

"Need something?" I asked.

He scooted, separating our shoulders.

Why did that make me feel…emptier?

He looked down at his hands. If I didn't know him better, I would've thought he was nervous about something. This man *never* lacked self-confidence.

Then he lowered his voice so only I could hear. "I just…I don't know…wanted to be up here with you, see what you were doing."

My pen hit the bus floor and rolled beneath the

seat in front of me. I somehow kept the papers of his speech from following.

"Uh, okay. Well, that's cool, I guess. Hi."

I'm such an idiot.

He smiled—not the practiced, plastic gesture he gave the public. This was sunlight in a bottle bright, and it crested just above his eyes.

"Hi back," he said, like a cute fucking kindergartner.

My mouth was suddenly parched, and sweat beaded around my collar. I tugged at it, desperate for air.

His lips parted, ever so slightly, as he noticed my reaction.

He held my eyes for a gut-churning moment, then his face sobered. "Thank you for coming with me into the hospital."

I fidgeted, thankful to be free of the sunlight. "Thanks for inviting me. That was…something."

He didn't poke fun at my lack of words, just nodded slowly. "Yeah, it always is."

"Why don't you let people see you like that?"

"What do you mean?"

I shuffled in my seat to face him. "David, I didn't know that side of you existed. I mean, the man I saw in that hospital…he was…*shit*."

He barked a laugh. "I was shit?"

"No, no. Please. I didn't mean—"

"Please, I want to know. I *need* to know what you saw."

I searched his face and found only sincerity. He really did want to know what I had seen, what I thought.

"I saw a man filled with empathy, a soldier who had seen far too much pain and loss, a *leader* who feels the depth of his decisions and cares for those in his charge." I paused. "There were no cameras. You barred them. This wasn't about the campaign, or your image, or anything but comforting those who had sacrificed and might give more still."

His eyes didn't leave mine, though I saw a hint of moisture gathering.

"David, that's a guy I would follow anywhere, anytime, someone I would run through walls or fire for."

"Really?" His voice trembled.

I nodded. "It felt like I was meeting you for the first time, seeing who you *really* are under all this." I waved my hand around at the bus, then up and down his perfectly pressed shirt.

His smile returned, and damn if it didn't brighten the bus. "You think my shirt is too much? It hides who I am? Should I wear a tighter one? Or I can just take it off if you think I'll get more votes."

I jabbed him with an elbow and laughed. "And there he is again."

"Sailor," he said.

"What?"

"You called me a soldier. I'm a sailor. Don't ever call me a grunt again."

It took a second to register, then we both laughed.

I fished beneath the seat for my pen and snuck a peek out the corner of my eye.

David sat back in his seat with a sigh. His lips were upturned, and his eyes rested at some indistinct point on the bus's ceiling.

16

16

GO VOLS!

DAVID

The home of the Tennessee Volunteers welcomed us in a flurry of orange and white. Most cities hid their construction barrels as soon as roadwork was complete, but not Knoxville. The barrels' colors happened to match that of the home team, so the city proudly displayed as many of them as possible on either side of the interstate as one entered the city. Billboards normally agnostic to education were framed in Vol colors. A few even had orange-and-white flags flapping in the wind above them.

We didn't enter gates or a fancy tree line demarking the university's bounds so much as crossed an imaginary line in the city where student apartments and academic buildings slowly replaced offices and restaurants. The campus where more than twenty-four thousand students matriculated sprawled like spilled milk across a floor.

The bus turned into the section where athletic facilities dominated, then pulled up to the entrance of the Thompson-Boling Arena. This was the building where legendary basketball coach Pat Summitt led teams to win eight national titles. She grew up on a dairy farm and eventually played on the US Olympic team before turning her immense talents to coaching. In 2000, she was declared Naismith Women's College Coach of the Century. In 2012, she was awarded the Presidential Medal of Freedom. In my mind, she was the greatest coach the sport had ever known, and the void left by her passing would never be filled.

It was surreal to walk into *her* house.

As I led our pack of politicos into the gymnasium, walls filled with photos of her greeted us. When we entered the court, and an impressive row of National Champion banners looked down, a sense of wonder and history nearly overcame me. I was usually pretty good at keeping my emotions in check, especially before an event, but there was something special about walking through the tunnel and entering the court where Pat had reigned. I made a mental note to ask the campaign photographer to snap a few extra photos for my personal collection.

The sound of thousands of people chatting and

laughing jarred me out of my musing.

Students weren't known for following through on political activity, at least not all the way to casting a ballot, but we hoped to change that—at least enough to move the needle and win the primary. Even in ultra-conservative East Tennessee, the younger generation was more moderate on social issues than their seniors. I knew today could make or break our campaign.

"You ready?" Saul's grumble turned my head.

"Yeah. Go Vols. Rah-rah. That sort of thing."

He snorted in the way only a cynical old bastard could. "Let's not change the speech that much, okay?"

I grinned. "Yes, Dad. Mom already made revisions. I thought his pen was bleeding when I looked at the draft a couple hours ago."

It took Saul a second to realize I was teasing about Joe. We'd reached backstage, so he turned away and addressed a guy wearing a headset.

The crowd was louder than I'd expected, and the air seemed to crackle around us. I never got nervous. Never. Yet in that moment, I couldn't keep my eyes from darting and feet from shifting. Joe walked up and smiled. Somehow, that made my butterflies flap faster. What the hell?

"Did you read through the final version? It should be loaded into the prompter now."

I nodded. "Yeah, gave it two runs. Sounds good."

Joe reached up, and I nearly jumped onto the stage.

"Woah." He chuckled. "You're crooked."

He grabbed my tie and straightened it. I could smell the ham sandwich he'd eaten for lunch on his fingers. The closeness…damn, why did Joe being close like that—

"Shit, you're sweating," he said. "Let me get Deana."

He turned and darted back to where our staff was huddled. Half a minute later, our resident makeup artist, Deana, was dabbing my neck and cheeks, then messing with my hair to get every curl and lock exactly where it should be. She was actually our press secretary and far too skilled to be cleaning up my overreaction, but she insisted my image *was* her job. I'd learned it was useless to argue. She had more of a steel backbone than any of the stodgy old men I knew back in Washington.

Joe stood to the side, his eyes following Deana's hands and occasionally straying to meet mine. He caught me staring and looked away quickly. It was awkward—and cute—like a dog getting busted chewing a shoe. I didn't mean to smile. It just happened. Then his lips twitched, and I thought my chest would burst.

"Sir, are you alright?" Deana asked.

I startled. "Uh, yeah, fine. Why?"

She huffed. "I can't stop this sweat—and you're not even under the lights yet."

I chuckled. "I'm fine, Deana. It's just a little hot back here, and the crowd's got me kind of nervous."

"*You?* Nervous?" She smiled broadly and patted the upper part of my chest. "You're gonna do great. These kids love you. Just smile. We're behind you."

I gave her my best toothy flash. "Thanks, D. Really."

The voice of the Vols announcer boomed over the loudspeaker, "LET'S WELCOME…" I gulped in several deep breaths and ran my fingers through my hair. Old habit.

Joe grumbled behind me.

"What?"

"Stop messing up Deana's work. Hands by your sides," he snapped, though his smile belied his tone.

"Yes, Mom."

Joe started to say something, but the announcer finished his intro, and thousands of rowdy students roared. One final breath and I bounded onto the stage, waving a hand and smiling broadly as *Rocky Top* played. No self-respecting Volunteer sat during that song, even those rooting for my opponent. It was *their* national anthem, and a cheap way to get a standing ovation at the start of my speech.

17

THE ORANGE GLOW
JOE

The kids in orange and white ate David up.

Every time he flashed his pearly whites, squeals of unbridled estrogen soared above the crowd as several rows of sororities jumped and waved hands, hoping to attract the hot congressman's attention. That only encouraged his already healthy ego into bending down like a rock star and high-fiving anyone in range.

After the speech, we toured the campus, with a gaggle of gals in Greek-lettered jerseys and jackets trailing close behind. I thought David might've reached his adoration limit during the speech, but several girls—and a few boys—approached and asked for David's autograph. When one perky brunette bounced before him and asked him to sign her Zeta (which happened to be positioned precisely over her right nipple), Saul stumbled forward and offered her an autographed campaign flyer instead. She pooched her lip dramatically, then winked at David before darting back to the ever-present flock of Zetas on the sidewalk. David gave her a tiny wave as we strode away, eliciting a chorus of giggles and squeals.

I couldn't stop a grin. Being in David's orbit did that to people. I could see it now. Sure, he was still confident to the point of punchable, but I now knew it to be more a suit of armor than his true nature.

Our guides dragged us through the administration building, then a science center, then a library. I'd never been a big reader, and the *twenty-minute* tour of the university's stacks nearly put me to sleep. David did his thing, asking questions and appearing keenly interested in each aspect. I'd always thought one day I would run for office, but seeing the banality at play made me question that desire.

The sun was beginning to set. It seemed somehow appropriate that the orange glow of the waning sun would shroud the agriculture department as the day passed. Somewhere, I thought an English professor might be toasting irony. That made me chuckle.

"Something funny?"

For the second time that day, David made me jump. This time my notepad and pen went flying, one striking Saul squarely in the back.

"Hey!" he started and turned.

"Sorry," I said, rushing forward in a blush. "David startled me—"

"Always blaming the candidate. I see how this is." David couldn't resist a chance to kick me when I was down.

"No. I didn't mean—"

Saul laughed. "He's busting your balls, idiot. Grab that pen. The bus leaves in five."

Just like that, Saul turned and gave his best Yosemite Sam imitation and huffed away.

"Wow. He's all rainbows and unicorns."

David cocked his head.

I snorted. "Never mind. It's a…a kid thing." I nearly said a *gay* thing.

Sweet Jesus, that was a close one. Not that David would've cared, but I tried to keep my work life and personal life separate, especially considering the ruby-red nature of the grand division in which we stood.

David's eyes sparkled. He leaned in and whispered, "It's a *gay* thing too. You don't have to hide in this campaign. I'm proud to have you with me."

"Then why are we whispering?" I whispered back.

He laughed, a deep, rumbling belly laugh. "Good point. Do you want me to yell that, right here on campus? I will."

"No!" I said a little too loud, turning a few heads. I

lowered my voice. "Are you *trying* to commit campaign suicide in the heart of Trump country?"

He cocked a brow and shrugged. "I believe what I believe. They'll either elect me or they won't."

Without another word, he handed me my pen that he'd picked up and strode toward the bus. I stood there, staring like a stunned idiot, unable to move from the sidewalk that had apparently reached up and grabbed my feet.

DAVID AND SAUL ATTENDED A WHITE TABLECLOTH dinner with high-dollar donors while the rest of us settled on a Chili's near our hotel. *The boys*, as Deana referred to them between sips of her blue margarita, were dining on beef Wellington and sipping wine from a year and region none of us recognized. We, in contrast, munched on chips and salsa, and clapped like ten-year-olds when sizzling platters of fajitas arrived. We even lied and told the server it was Deana's birthday for the pleasure of her embarrassment when the waitstaff sang a birthday tune.

We had the more fun dinner—by a mile.

Around ten o'clock, the margarita wing of the party skipped into the hotel entrance. Yes, we *actually* skipped while singing "We're off to see the wizard…." What can I say, the gay force was strong with this one tonight.

Singular applause sounded after the final refrain —"the wonderful Wizard of Oz!"—and we whirled to find David and Saul, entering a few skips behind us. Our candidate, sharply dressed in his gazillion-dollar blue suit and silky red tie, was clapping and smiling broadly. Saul looked ready to pull a six-shooter out of an imaginary holster. He glared up as if we'd killed his pet parakeet.

Deana, more shitfaced than I'd ever seen her, hadn't turned to see the bosses, and tried to kick us into another chorus.

"We're off to see the—" She staggered a step. "Hey! Why'd you stop?"

Saul cleared his throat.

"Oh shi—" She turned and saw him, making an actual O with her mouth and holding it in place. That image alone was worth all the tequila in Tijuana.

David laughed.

Saul scowled.

Deana's compatriots unlocked their arms and fell to the lobby floor in drunken laughter.

She planted both fists on her hips and tried to sneer. It looked ridiculous and only fanned our laughter's flame.

"I'm gonna pee myself," I said through gasps.

"I can just see it: Staffer Shows Disgust by Showering Hotel Lobby," quipped Luke, our event coordinator.

My side was hurting, and my bladder pulsed. I tried to stand, but Luke slipped, and we both fell in a heap.

"Here, give me your hand." David's baritone drifted down to me, along with his meaty hand. I gripped it and let him pull me to my feet.

"Thanks. I'm sorry. I *really* have to pee."

I turned and bumped into the reservation desk.

Deana and Luke erupted. Tears flowed down both their cheeks.

"Joe!" Saul barked, ever the annoyed uncle.

David stepped over and gripped my arm. "Saul, go get some sleep. I've got this."

He gave David a questioning glance, then nodded once and headed toward the elevator.

"You two okay to get up to your rooms? Should I call 911?" David teased.

Deana and Luke stopped laughing long enough to assure him they were fine, claiming I was the only lightweight in the group.

I wanted to be offended, but they weren't wrong.

"Come on, let's get you to a restroom before Deana has to clean up a headline tomorrow."

"She'd be cleaning up the floor first," I said.

David nearly spat laughing. I could smell wine on his breath, so I leaned toward him and sniffed.

"That's fruity. How expensive was it? Was it good?" Then I realized my mouth was an inch from his and staggered back. "David, I'm so—"

"Come on, drunk boy. Let's get you to a bathroom." His eyes hadn't stopped smiling—or sparkling, or curling up, or whatever the fuck perfectly clear eyes did when they were amused. Damn, his eyes were *incredible*.

He half-dragged me to the elevator, swiped his hotel key, then kept me upright as we ascended eleven floors.

Eleven.

Wait. My room was on eight.

"Why are we going to eleven?" I asked.

He chuckled. "Do you even know what city you're in right now? Just trust me. It'll be fine."

Huh. Memphis. I mean Chattaboro. No, Knoxvegas. Dammit. I knew the answer.

The doors opened directly into a suite.

Fuck, that was cool. My room didn't have an elevator. And it was so bright. And there were flowers. Why didn't my room have flowers? Wait. The flowers were in a *sitting room* with fancy furniture. Why did Mr. Hottie Congressman get a sitting room?

"You have furniture," I said artfully.

He laughed again, then led me through the sitting room, into a bedroom with an oversized king mattress, then into a restroom.

I stopped cold, and he nearly fell over.

"You have a *hot tub*."

"Yeah."

"You have a fucking hot tub in your hotel room. I have a mini bar with Chex Mix."

He chuckled. "Do you have to pee or not? I'll get you Chex Mix if it'll help."

"Oh, right. Can't piddle on the fancy man's marble floor."

"No, you can't. Fancy man would be *most* displeased." His voice was so pretty and funny and sweet. I wanted to touch it. Wait. Can you touch a voice? I didn't know. I wanted to try.

David physically pointed me toward the toilet door and shoved me in. The door clicked shut behind me.

"David. It's dark in here."

I heard another laugh. "Turn the light on."

"Oh, right."

Shit, how many margaritas had I had?

I did my business, and my head cleared—a bit— enough to successfully turn the handle to the door and exit into the bathroom proper. David stood leaning against the vanity, tie loosened, arms folded, smile splitting his ridiculously perfect face.

"Stop it, okay?" I said.

His face contorted in confusion. "Uh, okay. What am I stopping?"

"Looking all handsome and muscly like that. *Asshole*. You're supposed to be an asshole, remember? I'm supposed to hate you still."

His head cocked like a golden retriever that'd been asked to go walkies. "You hate me?"

"No!" I nearly shouted. "Sorry, shhh. Not so loud, Joe."

There was a chair in the corner. He had a fucking chair in his bathroom. I threw myself into it, worried I might not be able to stand much longer.

"I did hate you. I mean, when you were an asshole. Not that you're not an asshole anymore, but I've seen you…in the hospital…and other places…not being an asshole. Fuck. It was so much easier when I hated you."

He closed the gap between us and squatted, one hand gripping the armrest I hadn't used. "What was easier?"

Damn, his gaze was intense. A ball of cotton or light or twirling barbed wire poked inside my chest. It tingled and hurt and burned…or something. My hand pressed against it, trying to make it still, but nothing worked.

"I…David…I can't explain. I mean…you're *the congressman,* and…well, my boss—"

I didn't get another word out because David leaned forward and pressed his lips against mine. He wasn't rough, but he wasn't gentle either. He *meant* to kiss me. He hadn't tripped and caught himself with my mouth or anything. I was pretty sure of that.

As startled as I was, I didn't dare move. Well, that's not true. My hand—the one on the other armrest—flew to the back of his head, and I kissed him back with all the margarita and salty chips I could muster. God, I'd wanted to kiss him for months. I could taste the sauce from his steak—and wine, I tasted *wine*—

I pulled back. "David—" I tried to protest.

He didn't speak. There was fire in his eyes, and I knew we were past the point of talking. He grabbed my face in both hands and pulled me toward him, into his mouth. I gave myself to him and melted into his arms.

It was five minutes—or twenty—when we pulled apart. There was hunger in David's eyes, and my whole body craved to press against his, to feel his heat and sweat and flesh. Then the last remaining sober brain cell in my head cried out and my eyes flew open.

"Oh shit," I said, hugging myself and pulling away from him as far as the bathroom chair would let me.

"What?" he whispered in a husky, *fucking sexy* breath.

"David, shit, I need to go to my room. We can't do this. *You* can't—"

His lips stopped my protests, but I pushed him back with both hands. Damn, his chest felt good.

"David, I've got to go. I'm sorry," I blurted out.

I stood and darted past him and into the elevator. As the doors closed, the last thing I saw was David leaning against the bathroom doorframe in a wrinkled blue shirt with an equally wrinkled expression.

18

CHATTANOOGA
DAVID

I didn't sit with Joe on the two-hour bus ride from Knoxville to Chattanooga. In fact, I didn't leave my curtained-off private quarters.

The funny thing was, all I wanted to do was see him, to look into his eyes and brush my hand against his cheek. After he ran out of my room last night, I couldn't shake him from my dreams. He was in all of them. When I woke, I saw him in the mirror next to me, shaving and getting ready for the day.

Dammit.

I was supposed to be past all these feelings. There hadn't been a single man who'd turned my head since—

Grabbing the papers on the seat beside me, I tried to focus on Revolutionary War heroes and how we honored them. That made me think of men in uniform, which made me think of Scott.

That just made me sad.

Fuck.

I tossed the papers down and grabbed my calendar. Reviewing our twenty-four hours in Chattanooga was sure to bore me out of my somber mood.

The day would begin with the editorial board of the local paper, *The Chattanooga Times Free Press*. Awesome. They hated me, and not just a little, in the way most newspapers disliked officeholders. This was a full-throated, red-faced, "I wish you were dead" type of hatred. I didn't love them much either.

With my moderate voting record in Congress, there was zero shot at winning their endorsement, but we had to try. Kissing their ring was more about ensuring their support in the general since they *defi-nitely* wouldn't endorse the Democrat, the only people they hated more than me.

The next stop was a lunch with the local chapter of the Daughters of the American Revolution. DAR was extremely popular among the wealthy blue hairs who both funded and staffed political campaigns. Their volunteer hours were worth even more than their wallets—well, almost—and little old ladies loved me. I rarely did one of those events without my shirt smelling like expensive perfume and having lipstick stains marring its collar. Deana teased me incessantly every time.

In the afternoon, we'd tour a factory or plant. These events were hit or miss on the boredom scale. Occasionally, there would be a new tech or device that made the kid in me come out to play. Most of the time, we watched cows get fed, and I struggled to act interested.

The last event of the evening was another high-dollar fundraiser. Scribbled next to the calendar entry was a number twelve in parentheses, denoting the number of donors expected to attend. That meant tonight would be an intimate affair in which ridiculously wealthy people tried to pry information or influence out of a sitting member of Congress. The real game was to figure out which old fart was *really* a supporter, and which ones were playing both sides, donating to both candidates and priming the pump no matter who advanced to the general. Most of them did that. I tried not to take it personally, but to a candidate putting his professional life on the line, it felt disloyal.

I sighed. Politics. Nobody *made* me run.

The bus jerked and its brakes squealed as we pulled to a stop. I checked my watch. The noises of the staff standing, gathering their things, and chattering about the coming day drifted through my still-closed curtains. I tossed my calendar into my leather satchel and grabbed a blue-and-white-striped tie. The mirror Saul had stuck to the side of the bus helped me knot then straighten it. I tried to suppress the bus-seat-induced cowlick that rebelled against me, but it won.

Screw it. People liked candidates with flaws. Let them see Bessie's handiwork.

When the noise of the team exiting the bus quieted, I peeked through the curtains and ventured out. I wasn't sure why I was so intent on remaining cloistered, but leaving the confines of those curtains made me feel so…exposed.

Was that weird for a candidate running for governor?

Saul greeted me as I stepped off, handing me a fresh copy of the day's agenda. Nothing had changed, but he always gave me a clean copy to start the day. The man was diligent.

I scanned the staff as they straightened ties and donned coats. Joe stood at the far end of the pack and didn't look my way. He had the same cowlick. I couldn't suppress a grin.

"Something funny?" Saul asked, following my gaze.

"Oh, no, I was thinking about something from last night. I haven't had enough coffee this morning for anything to be funny yet."

He grunted at that. The man could down more coffee than anyone I'd ever met.

"You're the only one going into the *Times*. They won't even let me go in there, so good luck. If you're not out in an hour, I'll send in the National Guard."

I rolled my eyes. That was his standard line with virtually every event, especially those involving the media. Maybe he was less diligent than he was predictable—or *consistent*. Yeah, consistent.

Armed with talking-point memos and a watch, I left the safety of my clan and entered the news building. At least they'd have coffee.

Joe

I WATCHED DAVID WALK INTO THE LION'S DEN. Everything in me wanted to go wish him luck. Hell, I wanted to wrap my arms around him and kiss him for luck. The burn of his stubble from the night before still lingered on my lips. My fingers rose on their own to touch where his lips had pressed.

"Did somebody get some action on the trail?"

I whirled around to find Deana standing beside

me, a smirk pressing her lips together. I bet they didn't have stubble burn.

"Action, me? No, of course not. I mean…I can get action…but, um, no, I didn't. Not on the trail. Not here. No—"

"Hey, I was just teasing." Now she was eyeing me with suspicion. Shit. "Who were you thinking about just then? Come on, Joey, you can tell Mama D."

There were only two times when she called me Joey. First, when she wanted a scoop on some upcoming campaign activity. And second, when she wanted a scoop on my dating life, which had been basically non-existent, if one didn't count the mind-less yet regular sex with Sam. She loved hearing about close encounters of the Sam kind. I was her real-life erotica novel, and she refused to leave a single page unturned.

"Nobody. Really. I was just thinking…about the DAR speech."

She spat a laugh. "You were not thinking about little old women just then. Liar."

I gave her a sheepish look, but didn't respond.

"Fine. Keep your secrets for now. You'll tell me eventually. You always do." She started to walk away, then turned back. "If it's really juicy, I expect to be the first to hear about it. I have killed men for less."

I laughed. "You dodge to avoid killing ants on the sidewalk."

"Ants, I respect. Men, not so much. You've been warned." She winked and strode back to her briefcase.

I shook my head. What was I thinking? I had to be more careful.

Then I realized I was actually considering letting this continue—or start—or whatever. I wouldn't need to be careful if I did the responsible thing and kept my distance.

All I could think of was David kissing me, shoving me back into that chair, my hands on his chest, feeling the firmness of his muscles. I could still taste him. How was that even possible? His smell lingered in my nostrils. I wanted to run my fingers through his hair, mess every perfect fucking lock of it up, tear that cowlick to pieces and make it my own. I—

Shit.

I didn't know what to think. This was insane. David was straight *and* a congressman *and* running for governor. He was *my candidate* for governor. Rumors of him fooling around with guys were already rocking our ship. If we —

We couldn't. It couldn't. Whatever this was *couldn't.*

Fuck.

I wanted to…I wanted him to—

"Strategy session in five. The *Times* is letting us camp out in a conference room until David's done." Saul turned away without waiting for a reply. Why were people doing that today? What if I wanted to reply? Then I remembered what I was just mentally flogging myself for and thought it might be a good idea if I kept my mouth shut for a while.

Damn stubble burn.

David

"Then they asked me about gay marriage."

"What?" Saul leaned forward. "That's settled law. They were fishing."

I nodded. "Yeah."

"How did you answer?"

"By the book, like we rehearsed. It's settled law, and until the nine change their minds, there's nothing a congressman—and especially a governor—can do about it."

"They didn't accept that, did they?" Joe asked, his first question in thirty minutes of debrief.

I looked to him. A golf ball stuck in my throat as I tried to answer. "No. Uh…sorry, I need some water." I grabbed a bottle off the table and took a long sip. "They asked what I would do as governor if the court allowed states to make their own marriage laws. Would I protect traditional marriage, that sort of thing?"

"And your answer?" Saul asked, forcing my eyes away from Joe's. That took effort. I didn't want to look away from him. I was pretty sure he didn't want me to either.

"I told them that was a hypothetical, and I would assess our options if that day ever came. I told them the state had actual issues today that took precedence over anything hypothetical, and to come back to me when that issue was real."

Saul groaned. Joe looked down and avoided my gaze.

"What? That's true, isn't it?"

"You just went on the record saying gay marriage isn't a genuine issue. Every religious group in the state is going to pounce. Deana, get a clarification ready."

"On it." She scribbled furiously.

"Clarification? Why? I just told them the truth."

Saul's laugh was sardonic. "Truth. That's a good one, David. How long have you been in this game?"

I wanted to fight, to argue, but Saul was right. Shit. I'd just tossed the far right a softball, and the *Times* would surely pass that ball to whoever wanted it.

"Did they ask about Wayte at all?" Joe asked, saving me from the winding dark road of my mind.

"Uh, yeah. They asked how we differed on farm subsidies, the state income tax, biker helmet laws—"

"Biker helmets?" Joe choked a laugh.

"Yeah, it was a big deal years ago. Apparently, the biker lobby is asking the legislature to revoke mandatory helmets."

"And how do you and Shirley differ on such a vital matter?" Joe asked with a grin.

"Well, she thinks their heads are precious, and I want them to splatter all over the interstate."

"David!" Saul chided.

"Oh, stop. I'm teasing. We both oppose changing the law."

"So, they were making the point that you basically agree on every substantive issue, even the silly ones with no merit?" Joe asked.

I grinned and nodded in salute to his political acumen.

"Spot on. They're taking issues off the table and making this a *values* campaign."

"Fuck," Saul said, causing everyone to turn.

"Um, is that a statement or a request?" David joked.

"Idiot." Saul grimaced. "We'll *lose* a values fight, especially with your voting record. In Tennessee, there's no way we win that fight without photos of Shirley in bed with a small child." He thought a moment, then snapped his raptor gaze around the table. "Deana, get with legislative affairs. I want the top twenty pending bills in order of expense. Label them rural or urban, then mock up position papers and talking points. Get wonky. Joe, I need dirt on Shirley. Did she piss off someone at Sunday School? Cook fish in the office microwave? Hire an illegal to do work in her legislative office? I don't care how stupid it is, I want it."

He continued barking orders around the room, but my heart sank. We needed to set the agenda, to control the narrative, but our opponent was one step ahead. We were three months from the primary, and the skies were getting darker.

"Out, everyone. David and Joe, stay."

I'd tuned Saul out until that last order. My eyes snapped to Joe's. He shrugged, then looked down at his notes, though his page was blank.

When the three of us were alone, Saul barreled forward. "Joe, I've read your briefs on your sessions with David. It's time to wrap that up. Every minute we're not glad-handing or raising money, I want you two together finishing the candidate research. We need to be prepared for whatever the next attack will be. My guess, Shirley will fire with both barrels at the college rumors to knock you down for the count. Shit's about to get real."

Joe and I shared another look and nodded without looking away.

If Saul was right, we'd spend the rest of this campaign playing defense against allegations I knew were true.

Then my thoughts drifted closer to home. Were our glances obvious? Had anyone picked up on the chemistry between us? Fuck, there *was* chemistry between us. That was the first time I'd admitted it to myself. I snuck a peek. Joe was listening attentively to Saul as he droned on about other potential lines of attack.

I hoped Saul hadn't picked up on the shiver in the air between our eyes. It was like that effect they do in sci-fi movies when the space between characters shimmers and opens into a vortex. Yeah, Joe and I made a vortex.

Now I was thinking about Joe's vortex. I'd never seen it. I really wanted to.

Shit, this was bad.

19

THE DEEP DIVE

JOE

It took everything I had not to look back at David as we marched down the hallway toward my room. The little voice in my head kept repeating, *We're just going to work. We're gathering notes and going upstairs. Nothing is going to happen.*

I *wanted* to believe those things.

That wasn't exactly true. Every time David looked across the table and our eyes locked, I had to suppress a giddy shiver. Just his attention made me shudder. I'd dated a few guys before. Sam was my longest relationship, if that even counted as a relationship. Plenty of hotties got my blood pumping, but no one had sent me into unintelligible stupidity the way David had—the way David *did*.

This was going to be a long, uncomfortable night.

"This won't take a minute," I said over my shoulder as I swiped my room key.

"Uh-huh," David grunted.

I moved straight toward the bed and grabbed my satchel, then turned to the piles of paper.

"Shit," David said from the doorway before stepping to the bed. "We've still got to cover *all* this?"

"Yeah, I know."

He groaned. "I shouldn't have had that last drink."

I snatched the piles I knew would be the most challenging and stuffed them into the satchel. David walked around the bed to lean beside me and scan the pages of piles that remained.

The room was suddenly tiny—and hot.

"Are you nervous about something?" David asked in a raspy half-whisper.

When I glanced up, his face was inches from mine. I jerked back and bumped into the night stand, nearly knocking the lamp off.

"Nervous? Me? Uh, no. Why?"

He chuckled and closed the gap I'd created. "Since you're my priest now, I have a confession."

"Uh, okay. Should we talk about it upstairs… where there's more room?"

He grinned and nudged closer so our shirts brushed together. If I moved, our chests would—

"I can't stop thinking about you."

I froze. My mouth was a desert. I tried to look up, but my head wouldn't obey.

Then his fingers lifted my chin until our eyes met.

"Joe, I haven't felt this…well, it's been a long time."

"David—" I tried to protest, but his lips were suddenly pressed against mine, and the room tilted. My whole world tilted. There were no questions in his kiss. It was firm and sure, like he'd planned it, like he knew it was what he wanted.

My mind blurred, trying to wrap itself around whatever was happening, to make some sense of it, especially in the context of, well, everything. I knew I should pull away or push back or run—*something*—but I couldn't move. I didn't move. Then I realized, perhaps for the first time consciously, I wanted this.

I wanted *him*.

That thought made me nearly as dizzy as his kiss.

Our lips parted, and I finally breathed. How long it had been, I didn't know. I didn't care.

David stared into my eyes for a long moment before cupping my cheek and asking, "Was that okay?"

I nodded nervously, like some prepubescent teen who'd just been kissed for the first time.

He smiled.

Dammit. That smile was unfair.

It was the same smile he'd given thousands of times to thousands of people, and it was his most powerful weapon. And yet, in that moment, I knew it *wasn't* his campaign smile. It was David, unshielded and unguarded.

That smile was for me alone.

His other hand rose and he gripped my face, pulling me into him. I hadn't resisted before, but now I leaned into his embrace, kissing him back with all the pent-up passion and desire that had filled me over the past few months. He tasted of tonic and peppermint. It was the most delicious combination.

His hands fell away from my face as he wrapped his strong arms around my back and pulled me closer than I thought possible.

God, I felt…safe.

That didn't even make sense, but it's how I felt. I'd never felt that before. I barely knew what to think.

I really wasn't *thinking* at that point.

In some jujitsu move of the year, he wheeled our bodies around and positioned me above the rolling chair I'd been using earlier. It tried to scoot away as he lowered me into it, but stopped when it banged into the desk. As soon as I was safely seated, David's fingers began working on my buttons.

Our lips hadn't parted.

I tried to say something, but my mumble was buried beneath his tongue.

The first button unfastened, then the second. When the third gave way, he released my mouth and his head dropped, dragging tongue and teeth down my neck so slowly I thought he'd never reach my chest. I grabbed the back of his head with both hands and tangled my fingers in his perfect hair, kneading it into messiness like I'd done in my dreams the night before.

Tiny hairs on my chest tingled as he grazed them, then he flicked his tongue across my nipple. My head fell back. My whole body quaked. I'd always been sensitive, but damn—

David finished unbuttoning my shirt, untucked it, then leaned me forward to help remove it completely. His eyes traced their way down my semi-smooth torso, and he whistled appreciatively.

I let out a girlish giggle.

"Aww, is precious blushing?" the asshole said, looking up.

I grinned and looked away, unable to meet his eyes as my face blazed red.

"You're so fucking sexy. You know that, right?"

David's stare was intense. Sam said things like that, but they'd never meant more than "fuck me harder."

Why did it sound like so much *more* when David said it?

"Thanks," I said, two brain cells refusing to form a more coherent thought.

He chuckled. "And you're cute when you're flustered."

I turned redder.

His grin widened, then he looked behind him toward the bed. "Want help packing up your papers?"

"Papers? Uh, sure, yeah, we should, I guess."

He chuckled again and rose, then walked around so the bed was between us. I gaped up from the chair where he'd been undressing me a moment earlier. What was happening? Weren't we—

"We have a lot of work tonight, right? Better get your things together so we can start."

He reached into his pocket and tossed a room key on the bed, then turned and walked out the door, leaving me shirtless, breathless, and utterly perplexed.

***

AFTER A FEW MINUTES OF STARING BLANKLY AT THE door, I picked my shirt up off the floor and shook it out. When I held it up, I realized there was no way I could wear something that wrinkled in public. I might only be going with David up to his suite, but who knew who we might run into on the way? I changed into shorts and a UT T-shirt I'd picked up while on campus, then gathered my notes, careful to keep the piles organized. My hand landed on the stack I knew included David's sexual past, and hesitated. What was I doing? I already knew the answers, especially after what had just happened.

My lips tingled, still raw from the roughness of his scruff. A goofy grin parted my face before I scolded myself. This was a terrible idea. Nothing like this could happen again. Absolutely never, ever, ever.

Then I giggled.

I was *so* screwed.

I double-checked to make sure I hadn't left any notes on the desk or bed, then opened the door. David was leaning against the far hallway wall.

"I was about to send in the guard," he quipped, then scanned me up and down. "Nice shirt. Go Vols."

"Ha, ha." I rolled my eyes and turned toward the elevator, hoping he hadn't seen how rattled I still was.

He looked like the cat that ate the canary.

Being a canary was scary.

When the elevator delivered us to the penthouse suite, I raced into the sitting room and began laying out my piles. The restroom door clicked. I released the breath I hadn't known I'd been holding.

Twenty minutes had passed since I thought David

was going for the gold. Now, it looked like the jets had cooled and we were actually getting down to work. I wasn't sure if I was more relieved or frustrated we weren't *getting down* instead. The whole night had been one head-spinning moment after another, but I couldn't deny the excitement of it. I also couldn't deny how good David felt pressed against me. Sitting there, in his suite, I tried to focus on the task at hand, but all I could see were his lips as they drew closer.

Come on, Joe. Be a pro. Focus.

I chided myself and grabbed a stack labeled 'Moderate Votes in Congress.' Nothing killed a hard-on like a member's votes on farm legislation.

Then I chuckled at the silliness of a member making my member go down.

The restroom door squeaked, then a drawer slid open and shut. The rustle of clothing and…a belt buckle? I couldn't blame him for wanting to get out of his suit. It had been a long day—but all those images I'd neatly tucked away flared to the fore again. I imagined David stripping down in front of me. With each new sound from his bedroom, that piece of clothing fell away in my mind.

Dammit. I was getting hard again.

"Joe, you want something to drink?" he called out from the bedroom.

"Uh, sure. Yeah. Whatever. Bottle of water?" Why did this man make me stammer like an idiot?

"In the fridge. There's a mini bar in here too. Mind making some coffee? I'll need it if we're doing this all night."

The horny teenager in me giggled again. *He said doing it all night.* I was such a moron.

"Yeah, no problem. Where is that coffee maker?"

"It's back here, by the bathroom door."

I returned the papers I was reviewing to their appropriate pile, laid my pen atop the stack so I would remember where I left off. When I rounded the corner into the bedroom, there wasn't a bar to be seen. Only David, standing two feet away, completely naked.

His chest and abs were more defined than I'd imagined. He'd felt good through his shirt, but damn, he was stunning.

Despite my best effort at self-control, I roamed up and down his body, drinking in every drop of his six-foot-three, lean and muscular deliciousness.

His erection stole my breath.

"David, what—"

He stepped forward and pressed a finger to my lips.

"You'll have all night for questions after—"

"After?"

His other hand gripped the bottom of my T-shirt

and dragged it over my head, then he grabbed my bare shoulders and steered me into the wall. With his palms to either side of my head, he leaned forward and our lips met.

When he'd kissed me before, he'd been driven, his touch strong and powerful. Now, there was a softness, a gentleness I hadn't known he possessed. Ever so lightly, he pressed his lips, then drew them back, then dragged them across, sucking in my breath, until I ached for more.

"David, we can't—" I tried a breathless protest.

His chest brushed against mine and his cock, now pulsing, ground against my shorts. I moaned and forgot why I was objecting.

His mouth moved from my lips to my cheek, then he teased my ear with his teeth. He bit my lobe, and my whole body jerked.

"Sensitive, aren't you?" he asked in a devilish tone.

Then the fucker's fingers tickled my ribs and I doubled over. He dropped to the floor and dragged me down, tickling the whole way. Tears were streaming down my face before I got free of his evil digits. His grin was wider than I'd seen it before.

"I like it when you laugh," he said, smoothing my hair with his hand.

First, he's raging horny and slamming me into

walls. Now he's tickling me to tears and saying something sweet about my laugh? Who was this guy? I mean…damn.

At least I knew what to expect with Sam. On-schedule fucking. Simple and neat. Well, maybe not always neat, but simple.

What did David *want*? I cocked my head and waited for him to say something else, to give me direction for where this was headed. I was bewildered.

But I couldn't take my eyes off him.

He might've been the most beautiful man I'd ever seen. He definitely was the hottest man I'd seen naked. Part of me couldn't believe I was making out with a stunner like him. Then I remembered he was Mr. May in the Congressional Hottie Calendar and… hell, he's a *member of Congress*.

He cleared his throat, and my eyes snapped up.

"I'm over here. Hello? You know, the guy you were just grinding against?"

"I was…me, grinding? You…that was *you*," I sputtered.

He shrugged. "I might've ground a time or two." Then he looked down at my silky shorts. "I think he approves."

I pressed my head into his chest and laughed. "You're impossible. What the hell, David?"

He scooted over and his legs wrapped around mine,

then his arms around my shoulders. He pulled me into him and kissed me again. This time, there was tenderness and passion, mingled with desire. It took my breath.

I grabbed his head and gripped his hair like I'd done before. God, I liked his hair.

His hands trailed down my back, then dove beneath the band of my shorts to grip my ass. My body quaked at his touch.

In a flash, we moved from upright to sprawled across the floor, our legs still tangled, and his hands still exploring beneath my shorts. When he rolled me beneath him and something hard and uncomfortable stabbed into my back, I squirmed out of his grip.

"I think your shoe is trying to kill me. Can we move to the bed?"

He snatched the offending shoe and tossed it across the room, then did the last thing I expected. He pried his arms under my back and legs and hefted me up. Cradling me in his arms like a bride crossing a threshold, he kissed me again. Lips locked, he lowered me onto the bed and crawled on top of me. His weight pushed the air from my lungs, but I didn't care.

A moment later, he sat upright and stared down at me. His cock was twitching against my stomach.

"You're grinning," he said with a smirk.

"You look *okay*." I raised him a brow.

He snorted. "Yeah? Will I look better with your dick in my mouth?"

Without warning, he slid to the end of the bed, taking my shorts with him. My cock caught on the waist band and flapped against my stomach with a thud. He was on it before I could think, taking my full length all the way to the back of his throat.

"Fuck, David. Shit."

He grunted something, but his mouth was full, flicking his tongue as his lips moved up and down my shaft. One of his hands reached up and rubbed my chest and abs, while the other cupped my balls and drew them down, forcing my cock to stand even more upright.

"Holy shit, David. That feels—"

Then a finger teased my hole, and I nearly jumped out of the bed.

"Sorry," he said. "Too much? Don't like finger?" He actually sounded *nervous*. Mr. Cocky could be brought to heel after all.

I shook myself free of the trembling sensation. "No, I like it. You just surprised me."

He grinned at that. "I like surprising you."

Again, with no fucking warning, David renewed his attack. Two hands gripped my legs, pulling them apart. His face dug hungrily into my crack. I couldn't stop squirming as his tongue found my hole and tickled its tender skin.

"Sweet—"

English left me as his tongue entered deeper than I thought a tongue could. My hands flew wide and gripped the sheets, as I arched my back to give him a better angle. As many times as Sam and I had fucked, he'd never eaten me out like this. Not like this.

Then David's hand grabbed my shaft and stroked me while his magic tongue cast its spell.

"I'm not going to last long if you keep doing that," I gasped.

His stroking froze, then his eyes rose above my balls to stare up at me. "We have to go all night, remember?"

I laughed. "Dumbass. I'm pretty sure this wasn't on Saul's agenda."

He stuck his index finger in his mouth, then wormed its tip into my hole. "Neither was this. Fuck the agenda."

"Daaaaamn," I groaned as my head fell back onto the pillow. "I want you fucking inside me."

David's head snapped up. "What? Really?"

"God, yes, David. Fuck me. Please."

He leapt off the bed and sprinted into the bathroom. I was somehow reassured when it took him a minute of digging through his toiletries before he returned. He hadn't planned this—with me or anyone else.

I was also thrilled to see the trek to and from the bathroom hadn't softened his…resolve. A cock nearly as impressive as his rock-hard swimmer's build bounced toward me.

"Fuck, your dick is pretty."

David Reese actually blushed.

"I hope you like…I mean, I guess—"

He was so freakin' cute when he was flustered. "Shut up and fuck me, Congressman."

Fire blazed in his eyes at that, and he ripped the condom wrapper and tossed it to the floor.

"Let me do that," I said, reaching up.

Something about putting a rubber on my guy turned me on, no idea why. As it rolled over his tip, my mouth watered. I stopped and pulled the condom off, careful to keep it rolled, then took him in my mouth. He jerked so hard he nearly fell over.

"Fuuuuu—"

I wasn't gentle like he had been. I grabbed his balls and pulled them down, then gripped the base of his dick with my other hand while hoovering the shit out of his cock. His body spasmed every time I rose, then shivered when I went down. When I took the hand with his balls and craned a finger back to play with his hole, he lurched forward, and I tasted salti-ness on my tongue.

"Oh god. Stop. Fuck. I can't…fuck!"

I didn't stop. I drained every drop out of him, then released his balls and teased the slick head of his dick. It had that after-coming sensitivity that made the world shake with every touch. He pulled back.

"Joe, I'm sorry—"

"David, come here."

I patted the bed and he sat. I guided him down, then rose to my knees straddling him, his dick just beneath mine. He reached up and gently trailed his fingers from my chest down to my abs.

I squirted some of the lube he'd brought from the bathroom onto my dick and started stroking. His hand grabbed my wrist and pulled it away.

"Can I?" he asked.

I liked that he asked. It was very un-David of him. I nodded.

Two minutes later, he was coated in the fruits of his labor, and I lay by his side stroking his chest.

20

ACTING ON ORDERS

JOE

The day passed in a blur. While David and the team followed the carefully scripted agenda, I locked myself in my hotel room and outlined the next research session. Saul had made it clear we needed to wrap things up in the most thorough way possible. I wasn't sure speed and exhaustive research were friends, but they were the only cards we had left in our hand.

Campaigns *always* needed more time.

By seven o'clock, when I knew David and Saul would be midway through the main course with the fat cats, my stomach rumbled, and I realized I hadn't eaten all day. I scanned the notes stacked in neat piles on my bed. Each pile represented a line of attack, the issues and people involved, whatever information we already had on the issue, and additional background research needed. Because I'm an organized nerd, each pile was color coded with a RAG status based on severity of the attack. Green was low level. Amber commanded attention and a response. Red represented an attack that could take us down.

The final stack wasn't a stack—it was a notepad filled with questions I had for David. Twenty-two pages were filled with tightly packed, neatly lettered queries. A groan escaped as I realized how many hours lay before us—and that didn't count the dozens of hours of additional research left for the team.

Unable to stare at blue ink a moment longer, I tossed the question pad back onto the bed and slipped on my shoes. The hotel lobby had a decent sports bar, and their turkey burger was calling my name. I strode into The Ninth to find two members of our team sitting at a high-top table. A perky waitress had just set foaming mugs before them. They waved me over.

"Deana? What are you guys doing back?"

"The dinner started at five. We got done about thirty minutes ago." When I cocked my head, she chuckled. "You didn't read the agenda, did you?"

I shook my head and turned to get the waitress's attention. Before I had the chance, Saul's voice cut through the restaurant's jazzy music.

"Joe, we have a table in the corner."

I gave Deana a pleading look.

She grinned. "Sorry, kiddo. You'd better go. I'm scared of Saul."

"Yeah, me too. I just hope they're okay with me eating in front of them. I'm about to chew my own leg off."

"Give it a bite or two. They'll give in." She winked as I turned away.

David's striped tie from earlier in the day had been replaced with a solid blue one that nearly reflected the bar light. It hung loosely around his neck. He sat slumped in his chair with his head resting on the wall behind him.

"You look beat," I said as I sat.

Saul answered for him. "Doesn't matter. There is no *tired* until the primary is over. Then we sprint harder."

"Yes, coach. Whatever you say, coach," I teased.

Saul scowled.

"Sorry, just kidding," I said. "Can I order food, or do we have to be tired *and* hungry?"

"Go ahead, but we're working while you eat."

I glanced at David. "He's Mr. Sunshine tonight. What did you say at dinner?"

"Me? Why do you assume I said something wrong?" David sat up.

I rolled my eyes. "Because you're the only candidate we have. Oh, and you like to put your foot in your mouth at dinners."

"I do not!"

"Yeah, you do," Saul and I said in unison.

We chuckled while David groused and sat back with his arms folded.

"Are you ready to wrap up your candidate research? If we spend the next three months playing defense, we'll lose. I really need you moving into high speed on oppo so we can go on offense."

The server arrived and took my order, forcing Saul to wait impatiently. I caught David grinning as I pretended to look over the menu and asked questions about virtually every dish. The turkey burger was all I wanted, but it chapped Saul's hide that I was taking so long. That made it more fun.

When the server vanished, I dropped the menu on the table and said, "Everything's ready and laid out in my room. If you can carve out time in tomorrow's agenda, we can start in the morning."

Saul shook his head and stood. "No. There's no moving anything. You start tonight and go as long as it takes. Got it?"

I looked to David. He shrugged. "Uh, okay. Whatever you say, coach."

Saul rolled his eyes as he turned and walked away.

He muttered "I need a drink" just loud enough for us to hear.

The server appeared with David's vodka tonic and my iced tea.

David grabbed his glass and sucked down half the drink in one pull. He caught me staring and set his glass down.

"What? It's been a long day," he said.

I sipped my tea but didn't reply.

"You really like busting Saul's balls, don't you?" he asked.

"Not usually. He's a good guy—and an even better campaign manager—but everybody needs a little humility now and then."

He raised a brow. "Even me?"

I nearly spat my tea. "Especially you. Jesus, yes. *Definitely* you."

"Wow, thanks. You make me sound so…I don't know…full of myself."

"Let's just say, you're *supremely* confident." I raised my glass in salute and grinned.

His smile practically spread to his ears. Dimples the size of craters appeared. Next to his amused, twinkling eyes, they were the cutest things I'd seen all day. I looked down as a wave of heat rushed into my face.

His fucking smile widened further.

He leaned forward and whispered, "You're cute when you blush."

Now I did spit tea—all over his stupid smile and adorable dimples. Served him right!

"David!"

"What?"

I leaned in as he wiped his face with a napkin. "One, someone might hear you. You can't say things like that in public."

"And two?"

I sucked in a breath.

"Come on, there's always a two if there's a one," his vodka-fueled confidence intoned. "You're too uptight to violate the rules of outlining."

I leaned in further, my whisper urgent. "Two. What the hell? I mean, I know we…well, we…whatever. We can't talk down here. Dammit."

A part of me wanted to go with David's innuendo —even though he hadn't actually suggested anything —drag him by his shiny tie up to my room, and do things to make the voters blush. I could see my fingers unbuttoning his perfect blue shirt, slowly, one button at a time, revealing chiseled, smooth muscles while he nibbled my ear. I could feel his warm breath, smell his musk. I wanted his arms around me, his fingers gripping my—

Fuck, I either needed to drink more or less. I wasn't sure which.

This *had* to stop.

The server arrived with my burger and fries.

"I'm sorry," I said looking up. "Can I take this to my room? I need to get some work done."

The server nodded and vanished to box up my meal.

"Your place or mine?" David asked with a wry grin.

"David, stop!" I hissed. This man was *impossible*. "Seriously. Are you *trying* to lose this election?"

He held up both palms, but the grin didn't waver. "I thought it was a fair question. After all, Uncle Saul ordered us to work tonight. We have to do that some-where, and the only rooms available are yours and mine. I can't help it if you *misinterpreted* an innocent question."

"Innocent—?"

The server returned with my burger packed in Styrofoam and a check to sign.

"Fine. I'll gather my notes and come up to your suite."

He reached into his shirt pocket and waved his room key. "Nope. Won't work."

"Why not?"

"You can't get up to my floor without *my* key."

His face was all arrogant triumph. "So, I'll come with you to your room. You can gather your things, then we'll go upstairs to work in the sitting area of my suite."

I stared at him. He had that shit-eating grin I knew meant trouble, but I couldn't see a way around any of this. "Fine."

"Excellent." He nodded seriously, as if he'd just concluded Middle East peace talks.

I grabbed my dinner and headed off. The clatter of David's glass landing on the table one last time was followed by his chair scraping against the floor. Deana made eye contact as we passed.

"Saul's making us work. See you guys in the morning."

Deana's brows crinkled, then smoothed. "Okay. See you tomorrow."

David thanked them for their hard work. It sounded like he was shaking hands at a rope line.

I wanted to vomit.

My heart raced, and I could barely breathe, which was stupid. We were just going to work on research stuff. I'd done this a million times. There was *nothing* to be nervous about, but the idea of David coming into my hotel room was making me sweat through my shirt. At least his suite had a separate sitting area and kitchenette. We didn't even have to go into his bedroom. I didn't have those luxuries. He'd practically trip over my bed the moment he walked into my room.

Which didn't matter because we were just going to work.

Dammit.

Now images of David stumbling over my bed flashed into my mind. He'd reach up to brace himself, grip my arm, and pull me down with him. We'd slam together, our bodies tangled, our faces inches apart. He'd stare into my eyes. I'd swoon. He'd kiss me and—

I banged my knee against the last table before we left the bar.

"Ow!"

David's hand was on my arm in a flash. "You okay?"

"Shit, that hurt," I said, leaning with one hand on the offending table.

He didn't take his hand off my arm.

I didn't pull away.

When I straightened, he was standing in front of me, concern creasing his eyes.

"You sure you're okay? You smacked that corner pretty good."

"Yeah, I'm fine. Probably gonna have a nasty bruise tomorrow." I chuckled in a lame attempt to play it off, then looked down at his hand still gripping my arm.

That warmth in my chest flared.

He pulled back. Finally.

"Come on," was all I could think to say as I practically ran from his personal space toward the elevator.

21

QUESTIONS AND ANSWERS
DAVID

J oe woke an hour later. I'd stared at him while he slept. His mouth and nose twitched when he dreamed. It was adorable. For the first thirty minutes, he'd slept with his head on my chest and my arms holding him. His warm breath brushed my skin each time he exhaled. His hair smelled of fruit-scented shampoo and sweat. I couldn't keep my fingers out of it—or my lips. I didn't want to stop kissing him.

The logical part of my brain knew this was a terrible idea. I'd kept my attraction to guys at bay for years. Just the idea of being with another man put everything we'd worked so hard for at risk. Any shot at governor would evaporate. I could probably get appointed to someone's cabinet, but winning a race in Tennessee would be out of reach. With all that at stake, I'd still run headlong into him.

The funniest part of all this was how much he hated me when we first met. It was obvious. Saul even teased me about it. His banter was a little too pointed, his glare seething. His tone shifted abruptly when addressing me, from warm to professional-level ice.

I'd dreaded our first few sessions. They would've been painful regardless of who asked the questions, but Joe's perpetual scowl made things even less comfortable.

I wasn't sure, but I thought things had started to shift when we did the Campbell tour. I'd chalked it up to him being moved by the sight of wounded soldiers, but something in Joe softened toward me as well. His shell didn't exactly crack open, but his eyes held something more than loathing when they glanced my way.

Why did he drive me so crazy? It didn't make sense. Joe was cocky, annoyingly smart, and sent my blood pressure through the roof with his conde-scending glare. I knew his job was to push and prod, that he was there to get answers so we could win, but most people accepted my responses at face value. Nobody challenged what I told them—ever—until Joe. He'd seen through me and called bullshit. He hadn't even been intimidated by my office, and I knew this was his first statewide campaign. His whole pres-ence infuriated me.

And I couldn't get enough of him.

He was just nerdy enough to be awkward, but athletic and extroverted enough to cover it. His whole vibe made me weak. Even his arrogant posture when he was about to attack an issue revved my engine. And his smile—his smile haunted my thoughts.

I watched his eyes flicking back and forth as dreams drifted through his mind.

Watching him sleep made me smile. Hell, everything about him made me smile.

It had been years since a guy interested me. Sure, my head would turn when a hot, sweaty man walked by at the gym, but they didn't make me want to do anything beyond stare.

On the road, it had taken every ounce of strength I possessed to stay in my curtained cabin when I knew he was sitting by himself. He had notebooks full of questions for me, but I wanted to be the one asking and learning. He intrigued me, and I wanted to know more. I wanted to know everything.

Looking down at his sleeping form felt…I don't know. Hell. What was I doing? I ran my fingers through his hair again. I needed to feel him, to feel close to him.

Then his eyes opened.

"Hey," I said when he looked up.

He had that kid-who-just-woke-up look in his

eyes, and I thought I might die right there. I definitely couldn't suppress my goofy-ass grin.

"Hey." He smiled and nuzzled into me. His arms squeezed me, and my world swelled.

I kissed his head and held my lips there, unwilling to part.

"How long was I out?"

"About an hour. It's around two o'clock."

"Shit. Saul's going to kill us."

"You have world-shifting sex, wake up next to a Hollywood-level hottie, and your first thought is of Saul?" I asked in as cocky a tone as I could muster.

He slapped my chest and laughed. "Yep, still a full-of-shit asshole. At least you're consistent."

"Hey!"

He chuckled and surprised me with a kiss.

When our lips parted, he muttered, "I like cocky David, though I like David's cock more."

My eyes widened. "My cock likes you too."

He flopped back beside me and stared at the ceiling. After a moment, his grin tightened, and his eyes turned thoughtful.

"It scares me when you're thinking," I said, trying to make him smile again.

He didn't.

"Are the rumors about you and your college teammates true?"

I flopped back onto the pillow and mirrored his ceiling stare.

"Guess we're doing this."

He rolled onto his side, dug his elbow into the pillow, and held his head in one hand. His gaze now was wide awake and intense.

"There was *one* teammate, not three like they're saying. His name was Jake. Still is, I guess. I haven't talked to him since college."

"Was it a college experimentation thing? Or was it more?"

Images of Jake, his wild, curly blond hair poking out the sides and back of a blue baseball cap flashed. He had that smile too—almost exactly like Joe's. It made me weak.

"Yeah, it was. At first."

"At first?"

I blew out a breath. "We fooled around once in our sophomore year. It freaked us both out, so nothing happened again until junior year. We were pretty inseparable until graduation."

"You were *together* for a year and a half?" Joe sounded stunned.

"Two years, and I don't know if I'd use that word. *Together*. We hooked up a lot. I mean, we never labeled what we were doing. It was just sex. At least, I thought it was. Have you never seen somebody just for sex?"

I watched as something crossed Joe's face, some recognition. He knew what I meant, but like a dog with a bone, he wasn't letting go of his line of questioning.

"Jake is the guy saying you ditched him in college. He's saying you ignored your true feelings to pursue the dream of becoming president one day. I think the words he's using to describe himself are *political casualty*."

I laughed. "What a fucking martyr. That's ridiculous. I didn't even know I would run for office back then. We were kids playing baseball. Stupid, horny kids."

Joe hesitated.

"And after college?"

"I went into the navy."

"That's not what I'm asking," he said. "Were there any men in the navy?"

"Joe, I—"

He sat up and grabbed my hand and held it to his lips. It was the most intimate gesture I could imagine.

"David, talk to me. I'm not going to judge you." He looked down at our hands, then whispered, "Tell me about Scott."

"Scott? You mean—"

"Scott Winthrop, the SEAL from your team."

"Joe, please. Do we really have to talk about him?"

"You were in love with him, weren't you?"

I shot upright and jerked my hand away. I didn't mean to recoil, but a war between white-hot anger and deep pain suddenly waged in my mind. Panic welled in my chest and moisture formed at the corners of my eyes.

"What? *Scott?* Why would you say that?"

"Easy. Just breathe," Joe said. His hand rubbed circles across my back. His touch calmed me, and his compassion burst a dam I hadn't known was holding me back. A torrent of emotions flooded my chest, and I fell into him and willed his arms to wrap around me. When the sobs came, his embrace tightened, and I felt him kiss my head tenderly like I'd done to him earlier.

An eternity later, I pulled back. His hands still held my shoulders, then one cupped my cheek.

"You loved him, didn't you?" Joe whispered.

I nodded, unable to speak, not trusting my voice if I did.

A moment later, words tumbled out. "I *killed* him, Joe. He was the most beautiful person in the world, the kindest, most selfless man—and I killed him."

"No, you didn't."

"I did. I mean…yes, he committed suicide, but if I hadn't—"

The sobs returned.

Joe held me again.

Neither of us spoke for a long time. When my breathing slowed and shoulders stopped heaving, he ventured another question.

"You think it was the discharge that drove him to take his life?"

I stared into the past. "I don't know. Maybe. The story everybody knows isn't really what happened."

"What do you mean?"

"Scott and I were together for almost a year. None of the guys knew; at least, I don't think they did." I wiped my eyes and looked up. "I've never fallen for anybody like that. God, I loved him."

"But you got him discharged?"

It was a question, but felt like a dagger. "Yeah, well, it's not a simple signature, but I played my part. Scott insisted."

"What? He insisted? What do you mean?"

"The guys caught him rubbing my chest. That part's true. I'd been so startled at the time, it looked like I hadn't wanted him to touch me. It looked like I was pissed. The guys bought it, but they were dead-set on getting Scott out of our unit. I made that happen."

"Okay, but a simple transfer wouldn't get him kicked out, right?"

"No, but one of the guys wouldn't let it go.

He submitted a written statement that rolled uphill. Back then, that's all it took to get things started."

Joe's brows creased. "I'm still confused. What did Scott insist *you* do?"

"Everything. Kick him out of the unit. Sign onto the statement. Not object to the discharge. All of it."

"Why?"

"Because he knew it would blow back on me if I didn't. It would make it look like…like we—"

"Like you were together." Joe finished the sentence I couldn't.

I nodded slowly. "He took the fall so I wouldn't. He said it was stupid for *both* of us to get kicked out if we could help it."

"He must've loved you *so* much."

I nodded.

"Did you keep seeing him after the discharge?"

"I tried. God, I tried." I wiped fresh tears.

"You think they were watching?"

"Yeah. They were watching. Every fucking thing I did. I couldn't take a dump without one of the guys or some MP sneaking around."

"Damn."

"Yeah, but it was worse for Scott. His hometown was small. Everybody was in everybody else's business. He went from being the local hero to a cancer.

Four months after his discharge, I got a letter from him."

"What did he say?"

"Goodbye."

———

Joe

I HELD DAVID FOR ANOTHER THIRTY MINUTES AS HE cried fresh memories to life. I couldn't hold back tears of my own.

He finally looked up, red rimming his eyes. "Let's keep going. You need to know all this for the campaign…and because I *want* you to know."

I lifted him off my chest and sat up, trying to order my thoughts. I'd been so well prepared with my papers and questions, but there was no script for how this night had gone. After a moment, I decided to rip the last scab.

"What about Molly?"

"I loved her, but—"

"You were together three years before the accident?"

He nodded. "She was my best friend. We loved each other, but…I think she knew."

"Were there—"

"God, no. I never cheated on her. Never." He leaned back against the headboard and pulled a pillow to his chest. "We'd known each other since high school. She'd always been my best friend, the one everyone expected I'd marry one day. When we finally did, it felt right, like what was supposed to happen."

He stared into a corner.

"There was love, but no passion. I can count on one hand the number of times we had sex that last year. I mean, we loved being together, but there just wasn't any chemistry *that* way—and not just because I was attracted to guys. I know you're thinking that. We talked about *everything*. She didn't feel that drive either, at least not toward me. She said I felt like an old, soft robe that made her feel warm and safe, but that was it. I'm pretty sure she meant that as a compliment. Does that make any sense?"

I nodded, but didn't say anything.

"When she died…Shit, I can't—"

"Take your time."

"It's just…part of me was *relieved*. I know that's terrible, and I hate myself for it, but it's how I felt. I didn't have to live somebody else's lie anymore—and neither did she."

When I didn't speak, he went on. "That really makes me terrible, doesn't it? Joe, I loved her. She really was my best friend. I hate that I felt that way."

It took a minute for me to respond. This was too important, too personal, to speak without thinking. "I don't think anyone can judge what was right or wrong for you to feel, especially given *all* the feelings welling up inside you throughout those years."

He took a deep breath, then let it out. "I've never told anybody this—*any* of it."

I rubbed his arm. "And since Scott?"

He shook his head and offered a tight smile. "Only you."

22

___

THE RIDE HOME

JOE

The bus was pointed toward Nashville the next day. We still had several stops in smaller towns, but it felt good to be headed home. David and Saul stayed behind the curtain wall most of the day, which was fine with me. I had a folder full of notes to organize into a usable report, and I wanted a little space between David and I, just to breathe. He'd given me a lot to process.

Last night had been everything I'd imagined, though I never really thought it would happen. I hadn't bought David's "I'm totally straight" pitch, but I'd also expected a candidate for governor to keep it in his pants until after the election.

There had been tension between us from the beginning, but I'd thought it was more antipathy than attraction. He'd been such an arrogant ass, and I'd been, well, pretty hard on him in our sessions. It was my job to get answers, but I'd sharpened my knives more than usual. His swagger made me want to wipe the smirk off his face.

Who knew I'd end up doing that with my lips?

There was something else though, something that amazed me more than the fact we'd gotten naked. In my hottest dreams throughout the previous months, David used all the force and power I'd seen in him on stage. He was rough and strong, his lips hungry and aggressive, his cock slamming and driving like a jackhammer in cement.

Okay, maybe *that* dream was more a hope than expectation.

Reality had been different—at least, until things got hot and sweaty.

David was gentle. His kisses grazed more than pressed. His fingers caressed more than gripped. I could still feel his palm cupping my cheek with a feather's weight.

Without thinking, I reached up and felt where he had touched. My skin tingled at the memory.

Even in the throes of passion, David took his time and focused on making me happy, doing what he saw excited and pleased me. I replayed the night in my head. Never once did he ask for anything. He didn't tell me to *do this* or *suck that*. He was selfless in the same way—in the same way I'd witnessed in the hospital back at Fort Campbell.

I laughed at myself for comparing a sexual experience to a hospital visit, but it made a weird sort of sense. There was passion in his eyes, but also compassion. He wasn't getting off for the sake of it. He really was with me—*for me*.

That thought made my heart flutter and head spin all at once.

Nobody had ever rocked my world. Well, maybe Sam the last few times we hooked up. Normally, picturing Sam made my zipper stretch. He was hot as fuck, and was a *really* hot fuck. Sitting there on the bus, Sam's mental image did nothing, not even a tingle.

My mind shifted to see David, his eyes and smile bright as he waved from a stage. My whole body responded. Little hairs on my arms stood at attention, and I felt warmth flood through every artery and vein. A smile forced its way onto my face.

What the hell? I was a successful twenty-eight-year-old professional—and I'd never been more confused.

"Hey." David dropped into the seat next to me. I nearly jumped out the window. It was closed, but I tried.

"Easy." He laughed. "Can't have tomorrow's

headline reading, 'Campaign Worker Jumps Out Bus to Avoid Candidate.'"

I sucked in a breath and huffed. "Sorry. You scared the shit out of me."

"Not the effect I hoped for, but I'll take it."

His teeth were on high glow. "You're such an asshole. You know that, right?"

He laughed again. "Yep. And you love me anyway."

His teeth disappeared as he realized what he'd just said. Then his head and voice lowered. "Uh, I didn't mean…you know. I was just teasing."

Now it was my turn to laugh. "Aww. He's such a sensitive soul. Isn't that cute?"

He shoved me with his shoulder. "Now who's the asshole?"

"Never said I wasn't." I shifted in my seat to face him. "Was there something you needed, or are we stopping for lunch? Saul is up my ass for this report. You know, the one we worked on all night last night that I haven't had time to compile?"

A devilish grin parted his lips. "All night?" he whispered in that sexy, throaty rasp that sent my blood raging.

I mouthed "stop." My eyes, practically bulging out of their sockets, darted around to see who might've overheard.

"There's six of us on a bus that seats forty, and nobody's sitting within three rows of each other," he whispered. "No one heard me."

"Still—"

He held his palms up. "Okay, okay. I'll act like I don't know you from now on. Good luck on your report."

He rose to head back to his private section. I looked up, and he winked before bracing himself on the seat back and walking away.

23

DEBATE PREP

JOE

Time was a funny thing in a campaign.

When a candidate first declared, the nine or ten months between that day and Election Day felt like years. It's like being a kid waiting for Christmas or a birthday all over again. Then, in a blink, only hours of voting remained before local newscasters relayed returns. I didn't know how the campaign fates sped up time, but their sense of humor was wicked. They loved watching us go from calm, confident professionals to ants racing around our hill in a panic.

And it's a rush.

In the weeks following our first bus tour, Saul had David's time scheduled in ten-minute increments. When David wasn't talking with the press or attending a function, his earbud was planted firmly in place so he could make that next fundraising call. Most of his days began at seven and rarely ended before ten or eleven. He slept in hotels far more than his own bed in Nashville.

Magically, he showed no signs of wear. How he avoided bags under his eyes or a hoarse voice, I'll never know. Most nights, he'd leave Saul's tender care and head straight for the gym, which meant his head didn't hit a pillow before midnight. The man was a machine.

Unfortunately, that schedule also meant we barely saw each other. We'd only managed to spend a few nights together in nearly a month. Most of those nights were spent naked and exploring each other's bodies. He surprised me on the second of those nights by tossing me onto the bed, flipping me onto my back, and bounding onto my cock. It happened so quickly, I hadn't had time to register that he had given me his ass—and that he'd done it without a condom. By his third bounce, my protests died in my throat, and all I could do was feel his body mingling with mine. We lay wrapped together after each of us was spent, and he insisted he'd thought things through.

"You're the only man I've been with since Scott, and that was years ago. I've had countless physicals, and every kind of medical exam you can imagine. The military is pretty good about that sort of thing."

"But you don't know *my* history, my status, do you?" I asked.

He bolted upright. "You're okay, aren't you? You're not—"

"No, I'm not. I'm clean and negative, but you didn't know that—and that's my point. You've got to be smarter about things. Promise me, please."

"I promise." Then his smile blinded me again. "Did we just have our first real conversation about… well, about *us*?"

I snorted. "I don't think that conversation was about any *us* that might exist. That was common sense you need to learn, mister."

"Yes, Mom. I will."

He said that like it was nothing, like what we'd done was perfectly normal. Maybe it was for people who lived in a disease-free world, but I didn't know any of those people. Then I realized he was naive in the ways of the Dark Side. He'd been with a couple of guys, but had never been part of—or even closely associated with—the gay community. He might intellectually know what he should or shouldn't do, but he'd never faced the consequences of poor choices in a society riddled with HIV.

Whether he was governor or congressman or plain ole citizen Dave—and whether or not we ever became more than whatever we were in that moment—he

needed to see with clear vision. He needed to understand. I resolved to help him understand.

Despite the seriousness of that conversation, we
woke in each other's arms, made breakfast and drank
coffee together, then headed in our separate cars to the
office. For fourteen blissful hours, I experienced what
it could be like with David without the press hounding
our every step—just us in my apartment, doing normal
things that normal people did.

In the weeks that followed, *everything* reminded
me of David. I couldn't escape his name or his image.
We were running a campaign to get him elected, after
all; but more than that, I saw him when I closed my
eyes. I watched him run his hands through his hair like
he was some wayward model whose air machine had
gone batty. That made me giggle.

Fuck. I giggled. I was so screwed.

He called me most nights before going to sleep
and texted occasionally when traveling between stops,
but it was a poor substitute for spending time together.

I came to crave his lips more than anything.

David Reese had gotten under my skin. It sounded
silly when I said it out loud, but there it was. Just
thinking about him made me smile.

No guy had ever done that to me.

I stared down at my iPhone, scrolling through our
text exchange from earlier in the week, and giggled

again at the way his name appeared. I hadn't changed it since the campaign first started, back when I thought he was Satan in a suit.

REP. ASSHOLE: HEY FUCKFACE.

ME: HEY ASSHOLE.

REP. ASSHOLE: WE REALLY NEED BETTER NICK-NAMES FOR EACH OTHER.

ME: REALLY? BUT YOURS FITS SO WELL.

REP. ASSHOLE: HA HA. ARE YOU PLAYING ALL WEEK OR IS THIS COMEDY GIG A ONE-NIGHT STAND?

ME: FOR A ONE-NIGHT STAND, YOU SURE COME BACK A LOT. I THINK I LOST THE CHANCE TO GET AWAY THAT QUICKLY.

REP. ASSHOLE: I'M A CONGRESSMAN ON APPRO-PRIATIONS AND INTEL. YOU COULD NEVER GET AWAY QUICKLY.

ME: WOW. YOU SURE KNOW HOW TO MAKE A GUY FEEL SPECIAL.

REP. ASSHOLE: YEAH, I'M GOOD LIKE THAT.

ME: AND YOU'RE GIVING UP ALL THAT POWER TO RUN LITTLE OLE TENNESSEE? SO MUCH FOR YOU BEING AS SMART AS YOU ARE PRETTY.

REP. ASSHOLE: ALL I HEARD WAS BLAH, BLAH, BLAH. THEN YOU CALLED ME PRETTY. THAT MADE ME ALL TINGLY.

ME: You're such an idiot. :)

Rep. Asshole: And you love me for it.

Rep. Asshole: Shit. I mean IT. You love IT. Not me. You love our banter. Dammit. I'm sorry. Ignore me.

Me: LOL, Prosecution rests. You're definitely an idiot.

Rep. Asshole: Guilty as charged. Hey, gotta go. Miss you.

My lips pulled so wide at him missing me that my cheeks started to hurt.

"What's got you grinning like a goofball, Peaches?" Carla handed me a cup of coffee and motioned toward the conference room. Peaches was the name she'd picked for me after my first week. I still didn't know why she'd chosen it or what it meant.

I shoved my phone into a pocket and grabbed the coffee. "Thanks. Guess I'm just in a good mood. No reason."

"Mm-hmm," she said, looking at me over her horn-rims. "You can't fool mama. It's a *man*, isn't it?"

"Uh, man? What? No."

"*Definitely* a man." She chuckled. "They used to make me stupid like that too. Good for you, Peaches.

Get you some. There ain't nothin' like a good D to put a smile on your face."

She cackled, then turned and strode into the conference room, leaving me with my mouth open and cheeks burning.

Seconds passed before I found the will to live again and joined her around the conference table. We were the only staffers attending Saul's meeting in person, as the other key players, including Saul and David, were on the road. A flat-screen TV wide enough to make any geek jealous consumed most of the wall. Carla and I sat beside each other and watched boxes pop open as each new staffer logged into the meeting. Saul and David finally appeared. They shared a box as they were sitting in an office together logged in through Saul's laptop.

"Listen up. This needs to be quick." Saul's voice commanded attention. "Big picture: Primary Day is in six weeks. Our internal polling is strong, but things will tighten as we get closer to August. Shirley is scared shitless of our boy and only agreed to *one* debate. We've got to knock that one out of the park. It's in two weeks, just before the start of early voting. Carla, let's work on clearing David's schedule for practice sessions. Joe, research is over. You're on debate prep now."

He went through another twenty minutes of

agenda items, allowing each department head to report, but my mind couldn't stop spinning. I loved debate prep almost as much as I enjoyed readying candidates for press conferences. Grilling a candidate over their past was one thing. Pretending to be their opponent and verbally sparring in a mock debate was a whole different level of adrenaline. Beyond the exercise itself, the substance of the sessions would be based on the work I'd done in candidate research. It was where we proved how good—or lacking—my research had been.

I was pumped.

Debate was my jam.

BY THE END OF OUR THIRD PRACTICE DEBATE, SAUL was pacing and red faced.

"This is a fucking disaster. I can't believe we've come this far with a solid lead, and we're going to fumble at the one-yard line."

David looked up from his notes. Two podiums were angled toward each other on a stage. He stood behind one, while I, representing our opponent, stood behind the other. He raised a brow, but didn't dare say anything when Saul was about to blow his stack.

I gave him the slightest shrug.

"You two. Stop whatever bullshit communication you're doing. Tomorrow night will decide the fate of this campaign, and I can't take a single sharp comment or joke. You got that?"

I nodded.

David smirked and said, "Yes, Captain Ahab."

"What the fu—" Saul stopped himself. I grinned at the cartoon steam puffing out his ears.

"What are you grinning at? He's the candidate. He gets to show his ass. You, I'll fire."

I lowered my head. Saul was hysterical when he was angry.

"Saul," David ventured. "Please tell us what was so terrible about that run-through? I thought it was our best yet."

Saul took two strides forward to stand at the base of the stage. He crossed his arms and glared up at David. Between his height—or lack thereof—and the three-foot stage, he looked tiny. Tiny and angry. I had to cover my mouth and turn aside.

"First, your answers on taxes sounded like something a third grader memorized out of his daddy's GOP playbook. I didn't believe a single thing you said would help me or my family. Second, when *Shirley* over there attacked your votes on abortion, you wavered. I walked away thinking you were actually *for* abortion, rather than against it. Finally, the gay questions made me want to suck a dick—and I don't like dick. What the hell, David? You act like you don't care that people are calling you a *fag*, that Shirley and her team are smearing your name all over the state. From what I just heard, you weren't really denying any of it, which may as well be an admission they'll play in every commercial from here to Election Day. Where's the killer I saw last month, the guy who answered a question with straight talk and didn't dick around?"

I couldn't hold back any more. A laugh slipped out of my hand, sounding more like a snort, but the damage was done. Saul's head snapped toward me, and fire blazed in his eyes.

"You. Out. Now." He pointed off stage. "I don't want to see you again today. You and sunshine over there are going to work on his answers tonight, and I expect a *perfect* performance tomorrow. It's our last practice before the real thing. Try to take it seriously."

With that edict, he wheeled like a tiny top and stormed out of the auditorium.

David and I burst out laughing.

"I love it when he calls you Shirley," David spat.

"Don't look at me. My performance was to die for. You're the idiot with the bad answers. You made Saul want dick. Really?"

"Just because I like killing babies and sucking

dick? Or should that be in reverse order? I get so confused on stage."

I doubled over. David had tears streaming down his cheeks.

"You really are terrible. Saul's right."

In a blink, David stood before my podium, a lecherous glint in his eye.

"Good thing you have to coach me tonight, huh?" he whispered.

We were the only people in the auditorium, but I couldn't stop scanning the room.

"David!" I hissed.

"I can't help it. I haven't spent five minutes alone with you in a week. I'm excited we get to spend the night together."

I raised a brow and pretended to be offended. "*Working.* We get to spend the evening working, Congressman Reese."

"I'll work something for sure." He chuckled. "Want to do Thai? I haven't seen Achara and Joah since we ate there months ago."

I smiled. "Sounds great. I need to run by my apartment first though. Meet you in thirty minutes?"

"It's a date," he said with a wink. When I scowled, he laughed and trotted off stage like a giddy puppy.

ACHARA GREETED US BENEATH THE TINKLING BELL OF the restaurant's entrance, wrapping David in a warm embrace, then turning to offer me the same. She stepped back and looked from David to me, and I swear one of her brows raised, though she hid it well.

"It's so good to see you two again. How is the campaign going?" she asked as we followed her to the same booth we'd sat in months before.

"Really well," David said. "Only a few weeks to go. We'll need every vote though."

She patted his cheek. "Oh, David. You know we vote early, as soon as they let us in. Joah would never miss pushing that button by your name."

"Thank you, *mae*. You're the best."

"And it's good to see you again, young man. You look so handsome together."

David choked on a sip of water. I threw my hands in the air in protest.

"Oh no, thank you, but we're not *together*. I mean, we're here together, but not like *that*. Like together. Am I making any sense?"

Her eyes danced. She giggled. "I understand perfectly. You're still handsome, both of you, apart *and* together." She gave my arm a pat and vanished into the back.

"Well, fuck," was all I could think to say.

David chuckled. "Breathe. We've never given her

—or anyone—any reason to think we're anything other than colleagues; a candidate and one of his senior staff. Besides, even if she suspected something, Achara and Joah are family. They'd sooner die than hurt me."

"I'm not worried about them intentionally hurting you." I scanned the tables and booths. "Her voice carries, and she's not as subtle as she thinks."

"You're too paranoid. Relax."

Joah appeared with a platter of spring rolls. "David, so good to see you again. And, so sorry, remind me your name."

"I'm Joe."

"Right, Joe. Welcome back. It's good to see you both." He set the platter on the table, then offered a slight bow. "Sorry, very busy tonight. I'll come back later."

With the first bite of spring roll, all worries about the day and who might be lurking in the next booth vanished. Before we knew it, our conversation flowed from the House to the Tennessee Titans, to making fun of Saul again. It felt good to just enjoy a night away from the campaign with David. It almost felt like we were two regular guys out for dinner.

Nearly an hour later, Achara returned with her heavenly mango dessert, and David quibbled over paying the bill. As usual, she won, and no money exchanged hands. I knew he'd leave a ridiculous amount of money under one of our plates before we left—and so did she. The haggling was more about the dance than the result, and it was a joy to watch.

As we reached the door, Achara gave us each another warm hug, then she reached up, gripped my cheeks with both hands, and pulled me down to her.

"Joe, be true to yourself, okay? Life will be brighter if you do."

She patted one cheek, then let me go. When I turned, David was smiling. She winked at him and out we went.

"What was that all about?" I asked.

"She loves me. I think she likes you—and she sees through all your efforts to disguise how you feel about me." He nudged my shoulder with his as we walked. "She wants us to be happy, and if that means facing things together, so be it."

I cocked my head. "You got all that out of what she said?"

He shrugged. "It was either that or she wanted us to order more spring rolls. I'll go with the first thing."

I shoved him playfully. "Fucking idiot asshole."

"Hey! New rule. You only get to call me *one* thing at a time, not three."

"First of all, *fucking* was used as an adjective and doesn't count. That makes two, not three. Second, if you'd only *be* one thing at a time, your new rule might work."

He reached up and gripped the back of my neck like he was going to pull me in for a kiss, then yanked his hand away.

That moment sent a thrill through me. We were in *public*. He couldn't do things like that. We couldn't. But damn, it had felt like every happy holiday rolled into one when he'd touched me. He caught me grinning, and I turned away to avoid whatever smartass remark he was about to make.

Instead, he whispered, "You make me happy too."

My heart nearly flew out of my chest. "David—"

"Shh. We're at the office. Get in your car and meet me at my condo. We have *work* to do, remember?"

I was still goofy-grinning and couldn't speak, so I nodded and waved. Like a stupid, gibbering idiot, I waved. He was standing right in front of me.

He gave me the brightest white-hot smile.

"See you in a few."

DAVID DIDN'T ASK. HE DIDN'T HINT. HE JUST grabbed me by my shirt, hauled me onto the couch, and ripped my shirt off. I spared a quick glance to mourn the massive tear that would never be repaired, then focused all my attention on the man wriggling out of his clothes in front of me.

"I love your body. Damn."

He grinned and kissed me while he fumbled with his slacks. "You used the L word that time."

"Asshole. I'm gay. I *love* muscles and abs. You have them. Nobody here loves David the man. Don't get all twisted."

He laughed, and his crisply pressed slacks flew so far they landed on his kitchen counter.

"I plan to get very twisted tonight," he growled.

My dick leapt to attention, and my skin blazed. When his undies followed his slacks, the sight of his hardened excitement sent a different jolt through my chest.

"Well, hello, beautiful. I've missed you," I said, dropping to my knees before he could take off his socks. My mouth swallowed his dick so fast he nearly tumbled backward.

"Oh damn," he said, forgetting his socks and planting his hands on my bobbing head. He shoved my head down and made me gag. I sucked in a breath before he pushed me back onto him.

There was no gentle caress that night. We were hungry—no, *starving*—for each other. There would be time for cuddling and tenderness later.

I gripped the base of David's shaft and jerked him

as my mouth raged up and down. He moaned, and I felt his body tense.

"Oh no you don't, SEAL. You don't come until I tell you to, understood?"

The bold authority in my voice surprised us both. His eyes brightened and blazed as his lips crept upward.

"Sir, yes, sir," he said.

At that, I grabbed his shoulders and shoved him toward the kitchen.

"What—"

"Hands on the counter. Now."

"Uh, okay."

"Okay what?" I barked.

"Okay, sir." I was sure I heard him grin.

When his palms were firmly rooted to the granite, I gave him his next order.

"Bend over and spread your legs."

He moaned in anticipation.

I trailed my fingers across his body, savoring the goosebumps that rose in their wake.

He wriggled when my fingers squeezed his round ass, then gripped to pull it apart. I didn't tease or prep. Those were things for amateurs. Tonight was about taking what I wanted and him loving it.

Without a word, I shot forward like a torpedo locked on its target. I threw my face between his cheeks and let my tongue spear into his hole. His body lurched as my tongue dug into him as deep as it could. His sweat flooded into me as the soapy taste of his freshly washed ass tickled my tongue.

"Oh holy fuck!" he called out.

I reached around and grabbed his dick.

He twitched, then flopped his body over the counter. I rammed my tongue deeper.

He shouted something unintelligible.

I jerked his dick.

His abs clenched. His asshole squeezed. I let his cock go, sat back, and replaced my tongue with the finger now coated in his slick pre-cum.

"Joe…fuck…holy crap."

"You like that?"

"God, yes. I want you so bad."

I worked a second finger inside him. He cried out again.

"You've got me, David. I'm all yours."

"I want that, Joe. Fuck, your fingers…damn…I want you, Joe. Only you. Please take me."

My brain knew it should do something other than finger his ass, but my dick was in charge of the mission. There would be no thinking. Thinking was for wimps.

My pants were within reach, and I pulled out a sample packet of lube I'd stashed in a pocket. David wanted all of me. He was about to get it—and he didn't even know it was coming.

While my fingers worked their magic, I coated my dick with wetness and gave it a stroke. I was so fucking hard. Then I pulled my fingers out and waited a second.

"Please put them back."

"Please what?"

"Please, sir. God, just put them back."

"Careful what you ask for."

And I shoved my dick into him as hard as I could.

He shouted a full-throated yell I thought might bring the neighbors, but neither of us cared.

"FUCK!" he yelled. "Fuck the shit out of me, please. Tear me open."

I had to admit to being a little surprised by that. I didn't know David liked it rough, but who was I to argue. I rammed into him again, then jerked out and pounded him again.

He whimpered and moaned, and his hands left the counter to reach behind and pull me into him. I held there, my cock deep inside him, our bodies pressed against each other and dripping with sweat.

"Joe, fuck." He craned his head back to kiss me.

Our lips locked and I fucked him slowly. He shivered.

"I'm falling for you, Joe. I can't hold back anymore."

My gut spasmed. Just the thought of him saying that got me close, but I didn't want to come.

"David…god, I'm close."

"Stop."

I froze. His lips met mine again as we stood locked together.

"I mean it. I'm falling for you. Please tell me—"

"David, you're such an idiot. I've been in love with you for weeks."

"Really?" If one could hear eyes popping, I heard it then.

"Yes. Now shut up and go into the bedroom. I want you inside me before I come."

I pulled out of him, expecting us to move, but he spun around and gripped my face in both hands and kissed me. The horny, hard-pounding aggression vanished, replaced by a passion I hadn't felt from him since we'd started fooling around. He poured himself into that kiss.

"David—"

"It's your turn to stop talking. No more *sirs*. I love you. You're *mine* now, and it's time I showed you that. Will you let me?"

The intensity in his eyes took my breath. All I could do was nod.

With another kiss, he gripped my hand and led me into the bedroom.

In our third hour before cracking the books, David took charge. His kisses were emotions; his touch, memories. When he entered me, his body was gentleness and affection.

I tried holding back at first, listening to my brain as it begged me to protect myself.

It was wasted effort.

David Reese poured himself into me. He held me closer than I thought possible, guiding himself deeper, beyond the physical, willing his beautiful soul into my heart.

For that frozen moment in time, there was no Joe. There was no David.

There was only *us*.

24

THE DEBATE

JOE

The stage's front edge was rounded and covered in red, white, and blue bunting. Podiums, almost exactly the same as the ones we'd used in practice sessions, rose from the dais on either side. Behind, Tennessee's tri-starred banner snapped across a stadium-sized screen.

Hundreds watched from awkward folding chairs, many more from comfortable recliners in their homes. I paced behind the curtain while Saul chewed what was left of his index finger's nail. David stood rock still, his eyes focused on his podium.

"Congressman David Reese," the moderator said, followed by polite applause. Most in the audience were media. They had to pretend to like everyone—or hate everyone, I wasn't sure which.

David nodded once to himself, then strode

forward. His electric smile beamed, and one hand rose to wave in greeting.

And then it began.

***

GOING INTO THE DEBATE, POLLING SHOWED US UP BY twelve points, a lead well outside the margin of error. Shirley's team had to attack. They had to do something to drive up our negatives and narrow the gap. We knew it was coming, and used our prep sessions to brace for it, but practicing with paint balls was never the same as facing live fire—and Shirley came armed to the teeth.

Questions in round one were focused on doing business in the state and how each candidate planned to shepherd the state's budget, encourage new jobs, and drive overall economic growth. As the most famous whiteboard in campaign history once read, It's the Economy, Stupid!

David gave powerful, well-considered answers, directly addressing each concern with logical solutions. The crowd responded well, their applause bouncing between polite and enthusiastic.

Shirley, however, only spent a few seconds of her two-minute time on the question asked, focusing the balance on how David was a traitor to the conservative cause. She attacked his voting record in Congress like a starving man would a steak, raising every conceivable issue where David strayed even slightly from the party line. It didn't matter if the question was about tax policy, Shirley attacked on abortion or gun rights or immigration, none of which were terribly relevant to the duties of the governor of Tennessee. No one ever accused primary voters of understanding —or caring about—political nuance. It was the same in both parties. The base wanted the most rabid believer in their faith, and Shirley was doing a masterful job of painting David as an apostate.

The first half ended, and everyone took a break to allow the television stations to earn a few bucks. David joined Saul and I on our side of backstage behind the curtain, while Shirley high-fived her team in plain view of the cameras before retreating to their side.

"Wow, she packs a punch," David said, giving me a weak smile.

"And she's laser-focused on point," Saul said. "No matter the question, she found her way back to *their* message. You did great answering what was asked, but you're taking a beating for being a conscientious candidate."

"I'm all ears if you have ideas how to duck her punches." Frustration sharpened his tone.

Without thinking, I rested a hand on David's arm.

He turned.

Saul glared.

I pulled back. "Whatever she does, don't punch back. I know that sounds crazy, but she's kept her hits above the belt. If you strike back, you'll look like a woman hater on TV. Just…try to show compassion in your answers where you strayed from the party."

Saul's frown eased. "He's right. Look for an opening and do just that."

David nodded. Before he could say anything, the hall lights flashed, calling him back on stage. He gave me a quick glance, so I nodded and said, "You've got this."

When his hands were again firmly planted on his podium, Saul leaned in and whispered in my ear. "Is there anything you need to tell me?"

I startled so badly I nearly jumped on stage. "You really are creepy sometimes, Saul. And no, not that I know of. Was there something specific?"

He crossed his stubby arms and glared at David. "I have a bad feeling about the second half. We're about to get kicked in the nuts. I can feel it."

I tried to chuckle, but it came out strangled. "Keep your nuts over there. David's a pro. He'll finish her tonight."

Saul grunted, but didn't look back at me.

"Welcome back, everyone." The moderator's warm voice echoed through the hall as the crowd quietened. "Candidates, the first half of our conversation was almost exclusively focused on economic issues. In our second half, we'll discuss cultural matters."

My butt puckered. I thought David's pants tucked up his hole a bit too. This was what we were afraid of: a whole section on conservative values.

Come on, David. Just get through this without losing too much blood, I thought.

"Congressman Reese, Ms. Wayte drew the first question in round one, so we'll start with you now."

David smiled and focused thoughtfully on the anchor.

"Congressman, Ms. Wayte's team has made your loyalty to conservative principles a cornerstone of her campaign. They cite many votes in Congress when you strayed from what your leadership asked of members. How do you respond to the concern that your values are out of alignment with those of most Tennesseans?"

I nearly whooped out loud at the question. *We get to respond to Shirley's attacks without looking like we're fighting her! Come on, David.*

"Thank you for that question, Phil. You're right, Ms. Wayte has made an issue of my voting record over the past few months. She attempted to do that over the past hour as well." He looked directly into the camera, just like we'd practiced. "Let me talk directly to those of you sitting on your couch, or making dinner, or caring for your children or elderly parents. Those votes were for you, not Ms. Wayte or the party. Those votes *protected* seniors and their ability to afford medications. They *protected* women and their right to healthcare of their choice. They *protected* children, particularly those who weren't blessed with wealthy families, so they could enjoy luxuries like decent meals and clothing without holes."

Some in the crowd chuckled at that line. My smile widened.

"The difference in this race is simple—and it's not what Ms. Wayte wants you to believe. This race is about choosing a governor who will put the needs of our people ahead of his or her own ambitions. It's about which of us will stand up, even against our own party—when it's *really* hard—because it's important and the right thing to do.

"I welcome Ms. Wayte's next attack. Pick any vote. Let's talk about it. When we're done, I'm confident the people will understand. They'll appreciate that my vote was cast with them in mind, and no one else."

As David released the camera's eye, the crowd

erupted. Moderator Phil shushed them—they weren't supposed to cheer—but no one listened. David had struck a nerve.

"Ms. Wayte. You have one minute to respond," Phil said when the crowd finally settled.

Unlike David, Shirley ignored the crowd and the camera, turning to face David with squared shoulders.

"Oh shit," slipped out of Saul's mouth.

"Mr. Reese." She refused to honor him with his title. "You claim to be one of the people, a man who votes with only their interests in mind. How do you explain eleven votes over the past term when you voted to allow innocent children to die?"

"Ms. Wayte, the debate rules don't allow you to ask questions of your opponent," Phil said before David's mouth opened.

"Whew." Saul breathed again. "Thank you, referee."

"No, it's okay, Phil. I offered to talk about any vote. Let *Shirley* ask whatever she likes."

"Fuck, fuck, fuckety fuck. This is bad. Fucking bad. This is so fucking bad." Saul repeated the phrase like he'd suddenly morphed into Rain Man.

I was holding my breath.

David ignored our counsel and silent pleas and plunged forward. "*Shirley*, I assume you're referring to my votes against restrictive laws banning abortions?"

"They're pro-*life*—"

"Yes, yes. We all know you can read a bumper sticker." The crowd shifted at his condescending tone. "Let's go deeper than a slogan, shall we?" David was getting more patronizing by the word. "Six of those bills would've banned abortion in *all* cases, with no exception for risk to the mother's life, rape, or incest. Three allowed for the mother's safety, but nothing else. The other bill imposed jail time to the woman for having the abortion. The question isn't how I could've voted against those bills; it's how anyone with a conscience could've voted *for* them."

"Wow. I think I just felt points drop from our lead. Yeah, there goes another one," Saul muttered, and shook his head. I'd never seen him so rattled.

Shirley grinned. "Phil, while Mr. Reese is feeling generous, I have another question."

"I think we should—" Phil tried to reassert control.

"Go ahead, *Shirley*. Ask away."

Saul turned his back to the stage and pressed both hands to his head.

"Thank you, Mr. Reese." She bowed her head in mock respect. "Why don't we skip the votes and go straight to what families sitting at home really understand."

"Sounds great," David said.

"When were you going to tell the people of Tennessee about the man you had a relationship with for nearly two years in college?"

A collective gasp rose from the crowd.

David grinned, but I could tell it was more a nervous twitch than humor.

"Shirley, I'm flattered you care so much about whether I'm single or not. I had no idea the electricity between us was attraction, but trust me, I'm not interested in married women."

Another gasp rose from the crowd, mixed with a tittering of laughter. This was the kind of drama that drove media ratings through the roof—and our polling numbers into the cellar.

Shirley actually laughed. "Oh, *David*, from what I've heard, you're not interested in women at all."

This was going downhill fast.

"Candidates, please." Phil finally grew a backbone. "Let's get back to the debate format we all agreed to."

David and Shirley glared at each other a minute longer, then turned to face Phil for his next query.

"Congressman, I'm not a fan of candidates asking each other questions in debates. It goes against a moderator's job security." Everyone chuckled at that. "However, my own newspaper has reported on allegations of your college relationship. Other outlets and papers have also weighed in with their own investigations. This isn't just something Ms. Wayte has asked about."

The room froze as everyone waited for the question to come.

"Congressman, did you have a two-year relationship with a male teammate while you were in college?"

David's neck was turning red. I could see sweat lining his collar. This evening was about to get a lot worse.

"Yes. Though I wouldn't characterize it the same way your paper—or my former teammate—has described it. Like many twenty-year-olds, we were curious and trying to figure out who we were. We experimented. I'm sorry my teammate now describes our parting as painful, but that's all it was."

"For *two years*? You *experimented* with the same man for two years? Really?" Shirley bellowed from her side of the stage.

David reddened and shifted behind his podium. "I know how that sounds, but it's not like we were together all the time or living together or anything."

"I can't watch anymore. This shit's all yours. Call

me when it's done," Saul huffed as he stormed out the back of the theater.

Then Shirley dropped her bomb.

"David, we were all young once. I'll grant you that —even though I never experimented with things that go against Christian values, like some." She gave the camera a motherly gaze with raised brows. "What about Scott Winthrop? Was he an experiment too?"

David's head snapped up faster than I could turn back toward the stage.

"What the hell did you just say?" David bellowed, causing a ripple of nervous energy to flow through the crowd.

"Congressman—" Phil tried to intervene.

"No, Phil, she's invoked the name of a SEAL who died following his service to this nation. I want to know where she's going. I want to see just how low she's willing to go for a political office."

Phil stared at David a moment, considering, then turned to Shirley. "Ms. Wayte?"

She looked like she'd just climbed the podium to receive her Olympic medal. He'd taken the bait.

"Mr. Reese, a member of your SEAL team has come forward with an interesting story. He says, in a *notarized* statement, that Scott Winthrop was discharged for moral turpitude; specifically, for being homosexual."

She paused and watched David fume. The crowd murmured.

"He further alleges that, while you signed a statement supporting Winthrop's discharge, you were actually in love with him at the time, that you were his lover. Is this true? Were you an experimenting twenty-year-old at that time too?"

David's body tensed. His fists balled and released, then balled again. For a moment, I thought he might race across the stage and do something beyond stupid. When he spoke, his voice was low, barely above a whisper. The venom it contained was palpable.

"Scott Winthrop was an outstanding SEAL and an even better man. He died by his own hand, discarded by the country and community he served. How dare you dishonor his service—and his memory. How *dare* you." He growled out that last statement.

I hoped the cameras didn't pick up on his quivering lip, but I was sure they did. Cameras missed nothing.

Shirley cocked her head, as if thinking. She threaded tones of disappointment in her voice, as though David was her son she'd caught lying.

"David, my question had nothing to do with Mr. Winthrop's service, which I'm sure we all agree was honorable, despite his *dis*honorable discharge. Nor was it about his death. You have my deepest sympathy for *your* loss." She paused again to allow her implication to sink in. "My question was about your second gay relationship—well, the second one we know about. I dare not ask if there's someone special now, say, *on your staff?*"

"You're *way* out of bounds, Shirley." David's voice trembled.

I thought I might throw up.

No one in the hall moved. They barely breathed as we waited for Shirley's next words.

"David, like you said earlier, none of this is about us. It's about the people of Tennessee. The people of Tennessee cherish families. We love our children. We *protect* them. When we sent you to Congress, we thought you shared those beliefs—*our* beliefs. Clearly, we were wrong."

Phil finally asserted himself. He resumed his back-and-forth questioning.

It didn't matter. No one was paying attention.

Shirley had scored a knockout.

25

POST-APOCOLYPSE
DAVID

By the time Joe knocked on my condo door, I was three whiskeys into a night of unplanned self-medication.

"Hey." I turned from the open door, unable to meet his eyes, then threw myself back onto the couch and stared out the wall-sized window.

"Hey."

The door clicked behind him, but I didn't hear his shoes striking the hardwood. When I turned, he was still standing in the doorway.

He didn't move. He just stood there and stared. He looked…disappointed.

My heart sank.

I wanted to be governor, to do all the things I was promising in speech after speech. Politics was a rush, but *doing the work* was my passion. Seeing someone's life improved because of something I did gave me more satisfaction than any title or office—but without winning the office, my ability to impact people would be limited.

I'd blown it. I'd let my people down.

Worse, I'd let *him* down.

"How bad is it?"

Joe shifted his stance and shoved a hand into a pocket. "We won't have polling for a few days, but the media is losing their minds. A buddy in Shirley's camp told me they've already ordered T-shirts and bumper stickers that read, 'Clearly, we were wrong.'"

"Wow. Shit." I fell back onto the couch and stared at the ceiling.

"Yeah, that about sums it up."

I hadn't heard Joe move from the doorway. The couch shifted when he sat, and the warmth of his hand flowed into me when he laid it on my leg. I needed that warmth. I needed *his* warmth.

"David," he whispered, despite the fact we were alone in my condo. "I think…Saul…we talked…shit."

"Just say it."

"We *were* up by twelve. Saul thinks the lead flipped, maybe worse. The national media started calling right before I left. The story will be all over CNN, MSNBC, and Fox News."

"Fox has never liked me. I've always been too far to the center."

"They're about to paint you a lot farther left."

"Yeah. Wait, you said the lead *flipped*, maybe worse—worse than a twenty-four-point swing in one night?"

His hand found mine, and our fingers interlaced. Moisture welled in his eyes.

"We don't think it will be *that* close now. Saul's phone hasn't stopped ringing since the cameras shut off. Donors are pulling out, big ones. They're shifting their contributions to Shirley, and—"

"Fuck. What else?"

"Some staff resigned. Carla, James, and Jackie." James was our press secretary and Jackie ran volunteer operations. "That's going to add fuel to the media fire."

"*Carla?* Saul's Carla? She's been with him for years. Shit, she joined this campaign for him more than me."

Joe nodded slowly. "They all said some version of, 'We can't work for a gay candidate and have a future in the party.'"

"Well, they're not wrong." Then something made my stomach sour even more. "Joe, this is gonna shit all over *your* career too, isn't it?"

He smiled for the first time that evening. "I'll be

fine. I'm already out. Campaigns know I'm the gay staffer when they hire me. Hell, some hire me so they can brag about how open and inclusive they are, even while they're shunning the gay community. Being associated with an asshole like *you* might hurt, but the gay thing will be fine."

I tried not to grin, but he had some magic hold over me. "Still calling me an asshole, even when I'm mortally wounded? Thanks a lot. I used to like you."

"I never liked you, Congressman Asshole."

We laughed, tentatively at first, then all the tension and emotion of the day flooded out, and I found myself doubled over on the floor in a fit of hysteria. Joe was right there with me, tears streaming down his face.

When we finally ran out of laughter and tears, we blew out long sighs in unison. That made us chuckle again, but thankfully, the laughter fairy kept her distance.

"First time I've felt good today. Thanks."

Joe grabbed my hand and raised it to his lips. "Today doesn't change how I feel about you. You know that, right?"

Had he been more worried about *us* than the missile I'd fired into the campaign? Joe was a pro. I expected he'd be pissed or fired up, maybe out for blood. I never dreamed his anxiety would be about what happens next with us.

"Joe, they know," I said.

He cocked his head.

"Shirley and her team. They know about *us*. She practically outed us on stage tonight. The funny thing is, she didn't have to. She knew I was already down for the count. She pulled that punch."

"In case she needs it later to end you for good."

I nodded. "Yeah. Probably."

"Smart strategy. Gotta hand it to her, she's good."

"Any idea how she found out?" I asked.

His eyes went distant, then returned to mine. "Could be anything or anyone. Someone in the campaign could've leaked a rumor, or some camera guy got lucky and snapped us walking to Achara's, or overheard us there. Who knows? We haven't flaunted ourselves, but we haven't exactly been discreet either."

"Yeah, guess so."

"And she could be bluffing, making up something to see if it sticks. She already had the other two stories *with* witnesses. This could've been a stab in the dark."

"Huh. Pretty nasty stab." I rubbed my chest, feeling the wound. "She'll be a powerful governor. I just wish her heart was as big as her balls."

Joe barked a laugh. "She does have low hangers."

"God, stop. Now I can't get the image of Shirley Wayte with a hairy sack dangling from the bottom of her dress out of my head. Thanks a lot."

He snorted again. "I'm here to serve, m'lord."

"Fuck you."

"Careful what you ask for."

I grinned despite everything. I'd just screwed up in front of millions of people, and this man still made me smile.

"So, did the Wizard of Oz have any thoughts on where we go from here?" I had to get the business out of the way or I'd never be able to focus on anything else.

"He says we stick to the schedule until internal polling comes back. Shouldn't be more than a couple days. He wanted to let the media circus run its course. The polling team will start banging the phones tomorrow morning."

"And if it's bad?"

"Well, I guess you'll have decisions to make." Joe paused. "Sorry, I know that's not helpful, but it's the truth."

"I know. Thanks for the candor. Glad I'm not on *that* calling team."

Joe nodded. "That would totally suck."

"Did you just say *totally*, as in Valley Girl *totally*?"

"I *totally* did, Congressman Dude."

We laughed again, then my gaze drifted.

"What?" Joe asked.

"I don't know. Guess it's a good thing this is an off year. I didn't have to give up my seat to run for governor. The party will probably put somebody up to primary me. That'll be a brutal race."

"Hmm. You're in a pretty purple district, but the base is the base. I'm not sure you'll be able to pull out the W against a ruby red."

"Fuck." I put my head in my hands again. "Maybe I should switch jerseys."

The air in the room stilled before Joe spoke. "Maybe you should."

"Shit, Joe, I was kidding."

"I'm not." He rested his hand on my back. "Think about it. You're a centrist. Your economic and governmental policies are right-leaning, but your social stances lean left. The whole not-straight thing endears you to some on the left, even if it loses some on the right. Maybe running as a Dem isn't such a bad idea. It might be closer to where your beliefs really are."

"My parents would rise from the grave to haunt me. We've ridden elephants since I was old enough to recite the Pledge of Allegiance."

"I get it, but…people change. The parties have changed too. Set aside the radicals in either party, the center has shifted." Joe's hand moved from my back to my hair. I loved it when he scratched my scalp. "Maybe this is all for nothing and you'll be governor—but it's something to think about."

"Yeah, I guess so." I leaned my head into his touch. "You've never run a campaign for a Dem, have you?"

He actually coughed. "Uh, no. Pros don't go both ways—at least not professionally."

"Would you?"

"Are you asking me professionally, or otherwise?"

I smirked. "Both. Either. Yes."

"I'll flip for you any time you ask, but you already know that, you horny fuck." His grin wrinkled the skin around his eyes in the cutest way. "Professionally, I don't know. I don't think I could run a blue campaign and then be accepted back into a red camp. It doesn't work that way. Trust is everything in this business."

I grunted agreement—I'd just tossed any trust I had with my party out the window. That made my stomach churn.

Joe lost himself in thought. A moment later, his distant voice asked, "You like being in Congress, don't you?"

"Yeah, I really do. It's frustrating, being one of four hundred thirty-five. There's only so much I can do without haggling for votes. I was really looking forward to being an executive for a change."

Joe smirked.

"What now?"

"I've seen your decision-making up close and personal. Maybe being checked by a few hundred colleagues is a good thing—for the rest of us, I mean. You're pretty crazy, you know?"

"Fuckface."

"Asshole."

I shoved him playfully and fumbled to my feet, then pulled him into me for a kiss before stepping back.

There was healing in that kiss.

"You hungry?" I asked. "It's late, but I'm starving, and I think my stomach has finally stopped doing backflips."

"Yeah. Haven't eaten all day. Thai again?"

"Sounds great."

Joe

I woke the next morning with one arm draped over David's lap. He was propped up on pillows with two remotes on the bed beside him. CNN and Fox were quietly chattering away on televisions mounted on the wall.

"Morning, sleepy head." He leaned down and kissed my forehead. A wave of comfort swept through me. I giggled.

He smiled. "Something funny?"

"Not funny, really. Just...amazing. I still can't believe—"

His mouth stopped whatever I was going to say.

Wolf Blitzer barked a promo for his afternoon show, causing us to part and turn toward the TV wall. David's race was among his three teaser headlines.

"You made Wolf? Wow. Mr. Big Time."

He groaned. "Yeah, right."

"How's the coverage been so far?"

"Well, they're not calling the race yet."

"Ouch. That bad?"

He pulled me up to lie with my back pressed into his chest. He wrapped his arms around me and set his chin on my head.

"It's terrible," he whispered. Pain laced each word. "Joe, I'm not coming back from this, am I?"

I gripped his arms. "Babe...I mean, David. Sorry, slipped."

"I like you calling me *babe*."

My head snapped as far around as it could while he held me against him. "Really?"

"Yeah. I like it a lot." He kissed my forehead again.

I sighed and nuzzled back into his chest.

"What were you going to say?" he asked.

"Oh. Well, I can't sugarcoat this. I'm pretty sure we're going to get crushed on Primary Day. Shirley isn't letting up—and she shouldn't. This is a winning issue for her. Stake-through-the-heart sort of thing."

"Great. Now I'm a vampire?"

"You *are* pretty good at sucking."

"Eww! Vampires suck blood."

"You suck, and my blood rages. That doesn't count?"

David's chest heaved with laughter. "I really hate you, you know that?"

I flipped around and kissed him passionately. "I hate you too...*babe*."

His hands gripped my face in the way I'd come to love, and he pulled me into him again.

Long, affectionate moments later, he pulled us apart and held my shoulders.

"Should I step aside? Clear the path for Shirley? It could win a few points with the party leadership and let her bank for the general."

"The banking part is real, but the points aren't. You're a damaged candidate to the state leadership now. If you step aside, do it for *you*, not them." I stood, needing to make my morning trek to the bathroom, then turned back to him. "You could make a private call to Shirley, pull your ad dollars, effectively suspend campaigning, but stay in the race to save face. That would let her declare victory over a sitting congressman on Primary Day and allow you to run through the tape. I'm not sure if one is better than the other, but at least you wouldn't feel like you'd quit."

David stared blankly at the TVs, so I padded into the bathroom to take care of business.

PRIMARY DAY

JOE

Over the next week, Shirley ground her six-inch heel into David's skull—metaphorically, of course. Her ad spend went through the roof, with commercials mocking David's integrity, honesty, and his commitment to traditional values. One ad even pictured him with a rainbow flag superimposed in the background.

David refused to respond. He didn't do a single interview. He wouldn't even release a statement to the press, despite hundreds of requests. Outlets from every major market in the country wanted the scoop on Rainbow Six, as one conservative station dubbed him, a mocking reference to the Tom Clancy title.

Our internal polling firm reported in over the weekend following the debate. Saul and I were sitting in his office when a young staffer brought us a sealed envelope that had arrived by courier. Saul ripped it open and scanned the contents.

"Well, shit."

"That sounds promising," I quipped.

He huffed. "Look for yourself."

I rose and took the printout. There were three pages of stats, but only the first page mattered.

Post-Debate Polling Report — Reese, David — TN Governor — GOP Primary

Conducted: July 13–15; Comp: June 13–17

1. Most Important Issues (Pick Multiple)

34% TRADITIONAL VALUES/FAMILY VALUES

28% State Income Tax/Taxes

25% Safety in Schools

21% Agricultural Policies/Farmland Support

15% Abortion/Right to Choose

7% Education

4% School Choice/Charter Schools

2% Immigration

1. Positive View of Candidates

David Reese27% (prev 61%)

Shirley Wayte44% (prev 36%)

1. **Negative View of Candidates**

David Reese58% (prev 32%)
Shirley Wayte 48% (prev 43%)

1. **If Election Held Today…**

David Reese31% (prev 49%)
Shirley Wayte45% (prev 35%)
Not Sure/Undecided24% (prev 16%)

"Well, statistically, there's still a chance," I said as I laid the report back on Saul's desk.

"Statistically, we're fucked. In twenty years of doing this, I've never seen the numbers flip so hard and so fast."

"Yeah, and we've driven Shirley's negatives up pretty high in the process. Think she'll be strong enough to win the general? The Dem didn't face a primary and has a crazy bank built up."

He tossed his reading glasses onto his desk. "That's worth discussing with David. Maybe seeing the numbers on paper will get him to act, or at least let us *do* something. Not responding is driving this further into the ground."

"Do you really think we should fight back? If there's no shot, why keep punching? We'll just weaken our own nominee." I'd always been loyal to the team. It felt wrong to fight a losing battle, especially when it might let the other team win the governorship. No one's ego was worth that.

"You think he should pull out?" Saul surprised me with that question. He'd been letting me into his inner circle, but that was a strategic call well above my pay grade. When I didn't answer, he said, "Look, Joe, I know you and David are…close."

My head snapped up.

He put his palms up. "Don't shoot. I'm not mad. Hell, you made him bearable at times I thought he might blow his stack. I might recommend every candidate get laid a few times from now on—just not… well, you know."

I couldn't stop a chuckle at Saul's awkwardness. He was trying—in a very Saul way—to be considerate.

"My personal opinion and my professional opinion happen to align on this. Yes, I think he should back down. At the very least, pull the plug and reroute resources to Shirley, while quietly riding out the primary. The team is more important than any one candidate."

He snorted. "Fucking idealist."

"Yeah. You haven't jaded me yet, but I give you points for trying. You're a crusty little bastard, you know that?"

His snort turned into a belly rumble that made me smile. "I take everything you said as a compliment—except the part about being little. I hate fucking short jokes."

"Who said I was talking about your height?"

His eyes widened, then he barked a laugh. "Get the fuck out of my office and bring David in here."

"Aye, aye, captain."

As I left Saul's office, I realized that was the first time he and I had joked like peers. I'd always been a junior staffer, several pegs down from the chief. We might not win this race, but I'd certainly learned a lot—and gained the respect of some serious heavyweights.

"You're smiling. Please tell me it's better than we thought." David's voice slapped me out of my musing.

"Uh, well—"

"Shit. Okay, let's get this over with."

We marched into Saul's office and took our seats across from his desk. Saul looked up, his readers trying desperately to slide off his nose.

"Here. You're a big boy. Read 'em and weep." He tossed the report to David.

David scanned the page, nodded once, then tossed the pages back. Without a word, he rose and headed for the door.

Saul and I gaped at each other.

"Uh, what do you want to do now?" Saul asked.

"Think," was all David said. He left the office and didn't return that day.

David

THE NEXT MORNING, SAUL GATHERED THE CAMPAIGN staff into the wide expanse of tables, chairs, and cubes. Most had worked in losing races and knew what meetings like this typically held. There was no electric buzz racing through the assembled team like there would normally be for an impromptu all-hands meeting. The mood was somber.

Saul and I appeared from the conference room. There was no cheering or applause. No one spoke. They just watched with wary eyes.

Saul stepped to the side where Joe and a few senior staffers stood, allowing me to take center stage alone. As I peered into the eyes of those who'd poured

the last six months of their lives into our campaign—
into *my* campaign—I'd never felt so alone. Their
stares held accusation, some resentment, others pity.
Those were the worst. I couldn't hold their gazes.

"I'm not going to drag this out. Given the shift in
the polls this week, there's no way we can be competitive, much less win the primary. Our state deserves a
governor who shares the people's vision for the future,
and Shirley Wayte will do an excellent job. I support
her one hundred percent, and ask each of you to
consider doing the same.

"As a result, we're suspending our campaign
efforts, effective immediately. Saul has already pulled
our media buys. He's still getting his arms around all
the other things that need to happen, and I'll leave
those details to him."

I fought back something tickling my throat and
drew a breath.

"I can't say thank you enough to each of you.
Many of you have been with me since I ran for
Congress that first time. Jesus, I was like baby Bambi
trying to walk."

"You still are," someone called out, breaking the
tension and causing laughter to ripple through the
room.

"Yes, I probably am." I looked to Joe. His face
was an unreadable mask. "I've run for office a few

times now. It always amazed me how much we learned each time—and how much there's left to learn. This campaign has been no different. I've never run statewide. It's so much…*more* than I expected. Sure, there's more people to meet and territory to cover, but we knew that going in. I hadn't expected the weight. No, that's not the right word. Gravity? No, *enormity*. Everything, even the tiniest decisions we made each day, were bigger and more impactful than anything we did in my congressional races."

I ran a hand through my hair and gathered my thoughts. It felt like I was starting to ramble and needed to get back on track.

"I guess what I'm saying is that I learned so much this time around. About Tennessee, about politics, about campaigning. And, most importantly, about *myself*." I turned and spoke directly to Joe. "I learned what's really important, not just to the people of our state, but to me. I love public service. My ego loves holding office. But my heart…"

Joe looked down, unable to maintain eye contact. When he looked back up, my eyes were ready to catch his again. He didn't look away this time. I felt everyone in the room turn to follow my gaze. Still, Joe didn't flinch or look away.

"My heart learned what's important, *who* is more important than any office or campaign or ambition.

I've made a lot of mistakes in my life; some cost more than I could ever repay. I won't be the asshole who does that again."

Joe's mouth quirked at that word. Mine mirrored his.

I turned back to the staff. "I'm still a member of Congress, and this isn't the last you've heard of me as a candidate, but next time, I will be true to myself, in every aspect of my life, and let the chips fall where they may. I hope each of you will join me again when the time comes, but I'll respect whatever decision you make. Thanks for everything."

Saul stepped forward and dispersed the crowd. "Thanks, everybody. Meeting for department heads in thirty minutes in the conference room. Everyone else, enjoy the rest of the day off."

* * *

I CALLED SHIRLEY LATER THAT DAY. SHE WAS gracious and thanked me for my magnanimity in stepping aside. She asked if I planned to run again for my congressional seat, hinting she might consider me for a position within her new state government if I found that of interest. I thanked her and politely declined. I would better serve the people of Tennessee as one of their representatives in Washington.

As soon as I hit the end call button, press releases streaked across screens, alerting the media to our campaign's "new direction." I couldn't help but laugh at that phrase. There was no direction in quitting. It was more like running into a cement wall.

Saul officially terminated the paid staff in another all-hands meeting the next day. It was expected, but still sad—the final nail in the coffin for a campaign that should've been victorious. We agreed to pay salaries for another two weeks, but couldn't justify spending donor money on a dead campaign after that.

The whole ordeal didn't really hit me until that weekend. I was sitting in my condo Saturday morning staring at images of Shirley waving triumphantly on both screens, while CNN's scrolling headlines read, "Wayte Sails into General after Reese's Gay Lovers Revealed." Something in that one sentence made emotions flow freely. The next thing I knew, I was balled up on my bed with tears staining my sheets and Joe's arms wrapped tightly around my shoulders.

He'd never left my side.

The night I'd given my final speech to the troops, he'd packed a bag and headed to my condo. I hadn't asked him to come, he just did. He knew I needed his presence, his support—his warmth—even if I had been too stupid to know it. I don't know what I would've done if he hadn't been there.

We'd expected the media circus to continue for a day or two, then focus their fangs on meatier, more viable candidates, but early voting opened the following week, and having my name remain on the ballot kept the story of past lovers on screens and front pages across the state.

Nothing sells like a good sex scandal.

The only day I surfaced from my condo to speak with reporters was when I went to vote. Joe walked behind me as I plastered on my best smile, rolled up my blue sleeves, and made sure every microphone heard me say I voted for Shirley. It was a gut punch, but I knew it was the right thing to do.

Sometimes, the bitter pill is the one that heals.

———

THAT NIGHT, AS SHIRLEY CELEBRATED WITH HER supporters in a hotel ballroom, Joe and I sat at our favorite table in Achara and Joah's restaurant.

"They really do have the best spring rolls in town. God, I could eat a truckload of these," Joe said, stuffing the last of a fifth roll into his mouth. How he ate like that and stayed fit was a wonder.

I saluted with my wine glass, then took a sip. "So." I hesitated, dreading this conversation. "The Speaker called me."

Joe nearly choked on his roll. "*The* Speaker? As in, the Speaker of the United States House of Representatives?"

I grinned. "That one, yeah. Don't sound so awed. I'm a congressman. She's the Speaker. Members talk to each other."

"Yeah, but she's third in line to the presidency. I mean…that's *so* cool."

"Cool isn't the word I'd use, but okay." I chuckled. "She…well, she…fuck, this is hard."

"She wants you to flip." It was a statement, not a question.

My eyes widened. He really was politically astute. "Yeah."

"What did you tell her?"

My wine glass was three-quarters full. I downed it like it was a shot.

"You told her you would, didn't you?" he asked, his eyes lasering into my soul.

I hesitated, then nodded, not trusting my voice to answer.

He sat back and blew out a breath. "Okay. Well… shit. Alright. That's done."

My insides were still roiling, and I'd had a few hours to process things. I could only imagine what was racing through Joe's mind. His eyes darted back and forth as his mind tried to catch up. After several minutes, he still hadn't looked up at me. That made me even more sick to my stomach. Was this about to damage—or completely ruin—the one thing I was sure of, the one thing that mattered more than everything else? Would Joe walk away to avoid the messy partisan issues of dating the enemy?

I caught Achara's eye and wiggled my glass at her. This conversation needed a lot more wine.

The whole time I waited for Achara, Joe stared into the distance and didn't speak. I couldn't handle watching him struggle anymore, so I stood. "I need to use the bathroom. Be right back."

He nodded absently.

A few minutes later, I dropped back into my seat and took a deep swig of my freshly poured wine. God bless Achara. She'd left the bottle.

Joe made eye contact at last. "David, I'm sorry. It's just…it's just a lot to take in. I mean, I kind of expected something like this, but it's different speculating what might happen and facing it when it actually occurs. You know?"

Now it was my turn to nod without speaking. I couldn't find words. Maybe there weren't any.

Joe spoke. "So, I guess the primary's officially over now."

I nodded. "Didn't happen how we wanted, but it's good to move on—move forward."

He grabbed his beer, drained the last of it, then filled his empty water glass with wine.

My hand ventured across the table. Joe's face lightened, and he twined his fingers with mine. For the first time in a dozen minutes, I breathed without my chest feeling like a truck was on it. He gave my hand a squeeze and I blew out my nerves.

"Joe, what are *you* going to do now? I'm sure campaigns have called. The only off-cycle general in Tennessee worth working is Shirley's race, but there have to be candidates in other states who are knocking on your door."

He sipped his wine, then set the glass down. "I've had a few calls."

My heart skipped a beat. I couldn't decide whether to be excited for him or sad at the thought of him leaving to work who-knows-where. "You're really good at this. Any campaign would be lucky to have you."

He untangled our fingers and wrapped both his hands around mine. The fingers of one hand began stroking my palm. I wasn't sure if he was comforting me or himself. He looked so…tentative? Afraid? No, he looked *anxious*.

With that realization, I suddenly noticed how his leg bounced under the table. It bobbed faster than an angry woodpecker on a roof. How had I not felt that before now? His eyes narrowed, then widened, as if they weren't sure how to settle. Even his fingers, now stroking my palm, trembled slightly as they rubbed.

"Babe? What is it? You can tell me anything. Hell, after everything I've told you, your secrets would be a welcome distraction."

"Asshole," he teased, and jabbed a finger into my palm in rebuke.

I flashed him a toothy grin.

"There is one campaign I'm kind of interested in. They reached out a few weeks ago."

I leaned back against the booth, pulling our hands apart. "Weeks ago? Before we'd even—"

"About the same time."

"Wow."

"Yeah. The campaign needs a pro. They're decent, but are gonna get hit hard next year. Somebody with oppo experience will really help them."

"Huh. The candidate?"

He shrugged and sat back, mirroring my posture.

"He's a lot. Known quantity, kind of full of himself, but what candidate isn't?"

I chuckled. "Fair point. What level?"

"Congressional."

"Good for you, Joe. You deserve a shot to really make it in this business."

He hesitated. I could tell there was more, but he

needed to say it in his own time. I sipped my wine to give him time. He grabbed his glass and downed a huge gulp.

"Easy tiger." I grinned. "You drove tonight, remember? And I'm already too messed up to drive home."

"Oh, right." Then he cocked his head and did the last thing I thought this put-together guy would do: he guzzled the second half of his glass and reached for the bottle again. "We'll call an Uber. I need this."

My eyes were saucers. "Shit, Joe. Did you commit to get Satan elected to office?"

He nearly spat wine at that. "Oh, he's pretty close."

I raised a brow.

"David, you're an idiot. An adorable fucking idiot. I'm talking about running *your* campaign. Some-body's got to keep you out of trouble, and after this race, very few would touch your sorry ass."

"Hey! Many admire my ass."

"Idiot. Moron. Asshole."

"That's Congressman Asshole—maybe Honorable Mr. Asshole. Either works."

"You're impossible!" Joe started laughing.

I didn't.

When he saw my expression, his mirth fell away.

"What? I hoped you'd be happy about this."

I looked down at my hands resting on the table. "Joe, I really care about you. You'd have to switch parties to work with me now. I can't let you throw your career away like that."

He smiled. "First, you don't get to *let* me do anything. I'm a big boy, and I can make my own mistakes, which working for you again would clearly be."

"Wha—"

"You deserved that. Just listen."

I closed my gaping maw and nodded.

"That's *so* much better." He seemed to have found his footing and was now enjoying the conversation. That's when I knew I was screwed. "Second, I don't care about you like you said you do about me."

My mouth fell open again.

He crossed his arms.

All the noises of the restaurant—the chatting customers, the tinkling doorbell, the cooks banging pots in the back—it all fell away. Silence descended, and I held my breath. Joe leaned forward.

"I *love* you, David. One hundred percent. No question. More than that, I believe in you, in who you are. I would follow you off the end of the earth. Changing parties and running your campaign is nothing compared to what I would give up to be with you."

My jaw wouldn't work. I mean, I knew we liked

each other…more than liked each other…but damn.

"Please say something." Joe's voice had lost its confidence and squeaked out as a plea.

"It just…I didn't think you felt…fuck, Joe, I'm so in love with you it hurts."

Moisture flooded his eyes, though I was surprised I could see it through the waterfall forming in my own. Our hands found each other again, and we leaned forward in unison. His eyes said more than his words just had, and my heart soared.

"It's about time you two opened your eyes." Achara had snuck up on ninja-like feet to stand by our table. She held the same watery joy ours did. Then I noticed Joah's hands gripping her belly. He stood behind her with his head on her shoulder as they both watched us.

"Hi," I said stupidly.

Joah giggled. "Hi, *Congressman Asshole*."

In his heavy Thai accent, that nickname made me laugh harder than anything that night. I looked up to see tears falling down Joe's cheeks. Achara leaned down and kissed my forehead, something she'd never done before.

"We like this one," she said, inclining her head toward Joe. "It's about time you saw what we do."

And just like that, Achara and Joah fled for the safety of their kitchen.

27

THE GOOD FIGHT

DAVID

J oe and I huddled on the couch with our arms tangled and fingers entwined. Achara and Joah were wrapped in their own Twister knot on a love seat to our right. Pete paced behind the couch, unable to still his jittery legs.

The anchors were about to announce the early returns.

The Speaker had cleared my path to the party nomination, despite me being the newly switched kid to the Democratic Party. She explained to local leaders, disappointed by her near order to support my candidacy, that no other member would ever switch if the party skewered them right after they "came into the light." One stubborn far-left candidate entered the primary against me, but was easily swept aside by the resources and volunteer machine of the party proper.

Now, we faced my old party in the general. Our last polling, completed four weeks earlier, right before early voting started, showed us up by two points, within the three-point margin of error.

It was close. Far too close.

"Oh… my… sweet… Jesus. Will they just count the damn votes already?" Pete said what we were all thinking in his *very* Pete way.

"I hate this part," I said to no one in particular.

Joe gave my arm a squeeze. "Never gets easier, does it?"

I leaned my head on his shoulder. "Maybe a little now that you're here with me."

"Is it too late to change my vote?" Joah asked his wife. "These two are going to make me sick if they keep this up. We were never that bad."

She slapped his chest playfully. "You are *still* that bad, dear one. You cry at tissue commercials."

He snorted. "I cannot help it if advertisers know how to pull my strings. Kleenex is from the devil, I tell you."

We all laughed, and the tension in the room eased. A little.

Everyone's attention turned back to the television, but my eyes strayed—first to Achara, then to Joah, then settling on Joe. An overwhelming peace wrapped itself in disbelief. How had I been so lucky? It wasn't that long ago that I'd felt alone, adrift. And yet, this *family* was everything to me now. They'd seen me through the darkest times, and now shared the joys— and nerves—of the happy ones. I couldn't imagine doing any of this without them.

Joe had been a rock. When skeptics within my new political home pounced, he was the first to defend me. His skill at building bridges within the campaign pro network were impressive, and he brought fresh voices to our side nearly every day. We celebrated our first year together on primary night. It wasn't techni- cally the right date, but we thought it more appropriate to use the political calendar for our special occasions.

"We have numbers coming in for the fifth district race between Nashville congressman David Reese and Republican challenger Chris Heath." The anchor's excited voice, combined with Joe's sudden, iron grip on my hand, snapped me out of my daydream. "Woah, looks like nearly half of the precincts in this hotly contested race just reported in. As you may recall, Congressman Reese switched parties after a failed bid for governor in which he was outed by his conserva- tive opponent, Governor Shirley Wayte."

"Will they ever let that go?" Achara snarled, her hackles flared in defense of me.

God, I loved that woman.

"Here we go. With approximately forty percent of

the votes counted, it looks like Heath takes the early lead by a razor's edge. With just over a hundred forty thousand votes counted, he leads by roughly two thousand votes."

Pete rounded the couch and flopped down beside me. "And you call me dramatic. Do you guys have to make things so freakin' close?"

I chuckled and elbowed my friend playfully. He gave me a peck on the cheek then rose and resumed his pacing.

The hacks went on to analyze which votes came from which precinct, and which precincts had yet to report. They gazed into their crystal ball and predicted the race would come down to the wire and was too close to call.

"How do you do this every two years, David? I think I might pee myself, and I am not even running for anything."

"Maybe you should be running *for the restroom*, my dear," Joah quipped.

Everyone froze, then his words sank in, and we all broke out in laughter. Achara stood to ensure she didn't have any nervous accidents.

At eleven twenty, the now familiar tones of the anchor returned.

"Quick, turn it up," Pete's voice wobbled as he began to hop excitedly.

"Folks, it's been a rollercoaster in the fifth district race between Reese and Heath. Our last tally had Heath up by just two hundred twelve votes out of more than two hundred thirty thousand. All we're waiting on now is the last batch of mail-in ballots to be counted, estimated at just under ten thousand. This is a remarkably tight race."

"I think I'm going to throw up," I said, as I paced in front of the couch. Joe pulled me back onto the couch, then wrapped his arm around me and held me tight.

A knock came at the door, and a familiar voice called out. "It's time to come down, folks. They're about to announce."

On cue, the anchor said, "Folks, keep watching this district here. When our control room makes the final call, it will flip from gray to either red or blue. Two hundred votes separate those two colors…"

28

THE INTRODUCTION

JOE

David hadn't released my hand since we'd left the suite twenty minutes earlier. I had to match his strides as he paced so we didn't separate. I was pretty sure he'd pull me along if I didn't go willingly.

Three campaigns had joined forces with the state party to rent the ballroom, creating an odd atmosphere of party faithful who would cheer anything, supporters of candidates who'd won that night who were half-drunk and elated, and supporters of losing candidates who were just half-drunk—maybe totally drunk.

Red, white, and blue streamers fluttered from the ceiling where netting held a thousand balloons. Loud music alternated between classic rock, nineties pop, and patriotic marching band tunes. There was no way to miss the political tone of the gathering.

An electric excitement born of anticipation and hope thrummed through the crowd. There was no feeling like that anywhere outside the world of an election night. It was oxygen—or, for the losing campaign, the last pulse of life. I could taste the energy, feel it in my bones. It made me want to jump and run and scream, all at the same time. From the pacing and death grip David had on my hand, he felt it too.

All the local candidates had declared victory or conceded throughout the night, and only David, the highest-ranking candidate in the room, was left to speak. It was an honor to be last—and the most nerve-racking thing in the world.

"No matter what happens, I'm proud of you." I pulled David in for one last kiss. He held me tight and pecked my forehead. I loved it when he did that.

"I love you so much. Thank you for always being here."

Whatever I was going to say died in my throat as a thousand raucous voices stilled. The announcement was being made, the color on the screen was being filled. We gripped each other tight and held our breaths.

I watched Marcus Sanchez approach the microphone. The crowd roared.

Pete wrapped his arms around me and squeezed.

"Ladies and gentlemen, a year ago, it was my honor to be introduced as the new mayor of Nashville by a man I've come to respect deeply. Tonight, I'm proud to return the favor. Join me in welcoming to the stage your current—and now *Democratic—* congressman from the fifth district of Tennessee, David Reese!"

The crowd erupted. Music blasted. A thousand balloons and twice as many streamers escaped their netting, and David strode on stage.

I watched him embrace Marcus, then Maria. He hadn't known I'd arranged for Marcus to introduce him. The last thing I wanted was for him to feel pressure to impress the good mayor on top of a day of election results. I couldn't hold back tears as I watched them on stage and knew I'd played a role in each of their successes.

Then David, the honorably re-elected Congressman Asshole, jumped in front of the microphone and bellowed, "I'm not doing this without you, Joe. Get up here!"

Maria was bawling by the time I reached her. She and Marcus wrapped me in a group hug, then I felt David's weight reach around all of us. He grabbed my hand as our hug released, then held it high in the air toward the crowd. Cheers erupted anew.

The love of the crowd was overwhelming. Then I looked up to find David staring at me.

My breath caught.

He kissed my hand and mouthed, "I love you."

For a heartbeat in time, my mind went to that dark, frightened place where a love like ours could never be accepted, certainly never embraced. It was one thing for people to know David was gay, or had been with a man—but to put that man on stage, to share him with everyone…

Then my sight resolved on David again.

His smile glowed. His eyes blazed. His courage struck me to my core.

And the crowd wiped away my fears with their deafening roar.

ALSO BY CASEY MORALES

Raised by Wolves Series

My Accidental First Date

My Next Date

My Wildest Date

My Dream Date

My Last Date